SLOW DANCE AT DUSK

A MATURE-AGE CHRISTIAN ROMANCE

JULIETTE DUNCAN

A SUNBURNED LAND - BOOK 4

PRAISE FOR "SLOW DANCE AT DUSK"

"This book was worth the wait. When things look impossible. That's when you allow God to work out the details. Josh and Stella are an amazing couple. The death of Julian was hard on everyone. God uses that for the good. Sean is another exam of God's love an redemption. I have truly enjoyed every book in this series and I'm looking forward to the next book. " ~ *Deb*

"This is another EXCEPTIONAL sample of Juliette Duncan's writing! This series is so riveting, I sat up one night, all night reading, just couldn't put it down! The characters, setting, everything is fantastic! " ~*Bobby*

"Juliette Duncan never disappoints. This is another beautifully written Christian Romance that inspires and uplifts the reader. It is all about family, Faith, healing, and growth. Can't wait to read more about this lovely family. Their story must continue!! " ~*Sharon*

"How many tissues did I go thru during this book? The author fluidly writes absolutely the grief cycle while still reassuring us we are surrounded by our heavenly arms. This has been such a good series" ~*Debbie*

FOREWORD

HELLO! Thank you for choosing to read this book - I hope you enjoy it and are blessed by it. Please note that this story is set in Australia, and Australian spelling and terminology have been used throughout.

Happy reading!
Juliette

BOOKS IN THIS SERIES

Slow Road to Love

Slow Path to Peace

Slow Ride Home

Slow Dance at Dusk

Slow Trek to Triumph

Christmas at Goddard Downs

Beneath the Southern Cross: Dawn of a Sunburned Land Series

Love's Unwavering Hope

Love's Rebellious Spirit

Love's Distant Dream

Love's Precious Moments

Love's Faithful Journey

CHAPTER 1

*L*ife had continued throwing curveballs at Joshua, but with Julian's death, he'd finally struck out. The games of his past were over. There was no looking back.

In the four months since his brother's body had been laid to rest in the family cemetery at Goddard Downs, life had fallen into a new routine. To the outsider, all might appear normal, but Julian's death echoed in the halls of the homestead and the hearts of all who lived there. Yet, despite the sadness, good had come.

The moment Joshua's gaze met Stella's at Julian's funeral, he knew everything between them was about to change. And it had. Their friendship had blossomed and transformed into something he'd never dreamed possible. She was no longer an unattainable desire of his heart, but someone willing to stand by his side as he battled his demons, of which there were plenty.

Facing the bitter, angry man he'd become hadn't been easy, but was necessary if he no longer wanted to drift. And that's what he wanted. He didn't want to go through life without direction or focus, chasing fleeting excitement that in the end meant nothing. He didn't want to be like his cousin Sean, but he couldn't become Julian, either. He had to be himself. But first, he had to find out who that was.

He'd once heard that the love of the right woman could change a man. He wasn't sure if that was true, but as he stood on the tarmac of the Kimberley Regional Airport helipad, gazing into Stella Martin's deep, brown eyes, he thought it could be. She'd entered his life by chance at a rodeo in Alice Springs several years earlier, and then returned to it recently when she came to Goddard Downs seeking work. Now, as the station's vet, she'd become more a part of his life than he ever imagined possible. It was almost as if she'd always been part of him.

"I wish I didn't have to go." She took hold of his hand as a gust of wind sent her blonde hair flying about her face. She brushed the strands back behind her ear with her other hand and smiled wistfully.

She was gorgeous, and the mere sight of her made Joshua's heart quicken. He squeezed her hand as a long breath left his lungs. "I wish you didn't either, but you have to. It's Christmas and your family needs you."

"I *could* go at the beginning of the year. I feel as if I'm abandoning you."

Her concern warmed his heart, and although he wanted her to stay at Goddard Downs for Christmas, he couldn't allow her to sacrifice that special time with her family. Since Julian's passing, Joshua had gained a new appreciation of family. His one regret was that it had taken him so long to arrive at this point. "I wouldn't want you to do that. This is the first time your entire family will be together for Christmas since before you were born. You can't miss that."

"I know, but I'm torn. Things between us are just beginning, and the rainy season is here, and the station needs every hand."

"The station can manage two weeks without you." He stepped forward and raised his hand to her cheek while gazing into her eyes. *But I'm not sure I can...* He cleared his throat. "And with regards to us, I'd say things are going just fine. Wouldn't you?"

She gave a smile that sent his pulse racing. Her smile emboldened him, and he felt stronger, like he could do anything if she were beside him.

He who finds a wife finds a good thing and obtains favour from God.

He blinked. *A wife?* Before Stella, he'd never had a steady girlfriend, let alone considered marriage. But this wasn't the first time that thought had come to him since meeting her.

"Are you okay, Joshua?" She looked at him with enlarged eyes.

His brow furrowed and he swallowed hard. "What makes you think I'm not?"

Taking hold of his other hand, she squeezed both gently. "I know you're still carrying guilt over Julian's death, and that you're still mourning." Her gaze softened. "I'm here for you if you ever need to talk."

It wasn't what he was thinking, but she was correct. He

hadn't spoken to anyone about the lingering guilt he carried over his brother's death. Everyone, even Janella, had assured him it wasn't his fault. No one blamed him, but he simply couldn't shake the feeling that if he hadn't been so hotheaded and blind when he'd rushed off to Kununurra, leaving the family in the lurch, then perhaps Julian wouldn't have gotten into that truck in such a state of mind and he'd still be alive.

"Joshua?" Stella squeezed his hands again. "I can see it in your eyes. Don't do that to yourself. What happened to Julian wasn't your fault. You know that. So did he."

Joshua nodded slowly. She was right. Julian knew. He remembered the feel of his brother's hand squeezing his as he lay in that hospital bed, connected to machines, barely hanging onto life. Joshua had made it to his bedside in time to ask for forgiveness and to say goodbye, but it was too late for them to ever be the brothers they should have been. So many wasted years. They'd caused such grief to their father and to their family. And to God.

He drew a deep breath and shook his head to push the memories away. "You should get going. You don't want to miss your flight."

"Are you chasing me away?" Stella's voice held a hint of amusement.

"I'd never do that." Stepping closer, he cupped her face with his hands and gazed into her eyes. "It took us long enough to get to this point."

She wrapped her arms around his waist and smiled. Although she was tall for a woman, he still towered over her by several inches.

"I'm going to miss you," she whispered, longing filling her voice.

"I already miss you," he replied. "But the sooner you go, the sooner you'll be back. I want you to enjoy this trip. Make the most of the time you have with your family. Make every second count."

She nodded. "Only if you promise to do the same."

"I promise." He lowered his mouth and brushed her lips gently before deepening the kiss. He couldn't bear the thought of being apart from her for two weeks, and when she finally stepped back, he felt the loss immediately.

"I'll call when I get to my parents' place," she said, picking up the small bag from the ground and hoisting it onto her back.

"I'll be waiting," he said, soaking in every inch of her.

She gave a quick smile and then walked away. If he wasn't mistaken, she had tears in her eyes.

As STELLA HEADED to the taxi stand, she stole several glances at Joshua. Although her lips still tingled from his kiss and the distinctive scent of his spicy cologne lingered in her nostrils, her heart felt as heavy as her feet.

Why was doing the right thing so hard? Spending Christmas with her family wasn't a chore, but if she were honest, she'd rather spend it at Goddard Downs. With Joshua.

Brushing the tear from her eye, she gave one last wave and hitched her bag higher. She'd packed lightly since she wouldn't be in Cootamundra long, just two weeks, and she had no special plans other than spending as much time with her family as she could. Some of her cousins on her mother's side she hadn't seen in years, and she was also keen to see first-hand how her parents were settling into their new home. Despite not wanting to go, she needed to.

Behind, the noise from the helipad as a helicopter landed was almost deafening as she crossed to where a taxi sat waiting. She greeted the driver, a middle-aged man of Middle Eastern appearance, and opening the back door, she stuffed her bag onto the seat before turning to give Joshua another wave. He was standing right where she'd left him, and he was so downright hot that the mere look of him made her knees go to jelly. Short dark hair, the smattering of whiskers on his chin, muscles rippling under his crisp white button-down shirt, sleeves rolled up and tucked into a pair of snugly fitted jeans.

When he raised a hand and smiled, she fought the temptation to grab her bag and run to him. *How had this happened?* Only five months earlier she'd been fighting the attraction, but now, having admitted their feelings for one another, it was as if there was no one else in the world who could match her so perfectly.

I'm going to miss you, Joshua Goddard. Lord, take care of him and the entire Goddard family while I'm away. May Your mercy and grace be upon them as they continue to mourn. May they see the light of Your love even in these difficult times, and may You show them the way forward.

She waved to Joshua one last time as the taxi drove off.

The Goddards would be well. They had faith in God and He would take care of them. Her family was the unknown quantity, and she had no idea what to expect when she arrived.

CHAPTER 2

When peace like a river attendeth my way,
When sorrows like sea billows roll;
Whatever my lot, thou hast taught me to say,
"It is well, it is well with my soul."

There was something in the air. A feeling deep inside her that for the past few days she'd been unable to shake. Maggie wasn't sure what it was, but this she knew, something good was about to happen.

A smile graced her lips as she unravelled the lights from the packaging in which they were stored. Christmas was her favourite time of year, and it was a big deal at Goddard Downs. It was a time when they got to take things a little slower, enjoy each other's company, and pull together to survive the harshness of the rainy season. This year, more than any other, the station needed that coming together.

Julian's death was foremost in the minds of all, but after four months since his passing, the initial shock was wearing off and everyone was coming to a sense of a new normal. However, this year's Christmas celebration would be different. This year, both hers and Frank's families would come together under one roof. Last year, her son Jeremy and his wife Emma had gone to Emma's parents, and Maggie's daughter Serena and Serena's new husband, David, had their owns plans as newlyweds. This year, everyone was making an effort to be together.

Maggie doubted that Julian would have ever anticipated his death could have such an effect on both his, and her, families. His passing had made everyone connected with him reassess their priorities and take stock of what and who was most important to them.

Maggie certainly had, and she realised that despite the difficulties of life, she would rather go through those difficulties with family around her than suffer them alone. She rarely thought what it would be like to have her children under her roof again since it was customary for children to grow up and move away. Except at Goddard Downs, where they grew up and returned. Or stayed put. If only she'd had such an opportunity to watch the lives of her children and grandchildren unfold before her, not as an observer from a distance.

It's different for us than it is for You, Lord. You watch us from right beside us. We often think of You as being far off, but You aren't. You're right by our side, seeing everything we do. It doesn't matter how difficult the circumstance, how bitter the pain. You're always there, giving comfort and strength. Thank You, Lord, that we have this time to be together, to not only celebrate the birth of Your Son but to celebrate the gift of family that You've given us.

Maggie lifted her gaze as the sound of a whirring engine grew louder, drowning out her thoughts. They were here!

Pushing up from the floor, she made her way outside and raised a hand over her eyes as the helicopter hovered overhead. The sun was bright and the day hot, but not for long. In the distance, dark clouds filled the horizon. A storm was brewing, and the weather reports forecasted flash flooding. A warning had been issued only an hour earlier to the residents of the Kimberley. Maggie was glad that Serena and David had decided to come with baby Oliver before lunch, and not in the afternoon.

"Is that them?" Jeremy called from the doorway, two-year-old Chloe on his hip. The child was sucking contently on a fruit bar, her little head nestled into the crook of his neck.

"Yes," Maggie answered. Jeremy and Emma had arrived with the children three days earlier, and in that time they had made themselves completely at home at Goddard Downs. Janella, Julian's widow, was grateful for the extra hands in the kitchen. Since Julian's death, she wasn't much in the mood for cooking, but she continued in her duty, putting the needs of the family above her grief. Maggie hoped that with everyone there it would ease her pain further and return the smile that had been absent from her face too long.

Maggie turned her gaze to the helicopter once more. It swayed sharply and her heart faltered for a moment, but there was nothing to worry about. Frank was skilled behind the stick of a helicopter and would get them safely to the ground.

The second the rotors stopped spinning Maggie rushed towards the helicopter. By the time she reached it, David and Frank had already jumped out, but Serena sat in the back, the small bundle that was Oliver curled securely against her body.

"Welcome!" Maggie's greeting was bright as she stepped up and kissed Serena's cheek before stealing a peek at Oliver. He was dressed in a teddy bear onesie and made her go to mush. "He's so precious, sweetheart."

"Tell me about it," Serena replied with a chuckle. "He keeps me up every night, but it's the best sleeplessness I've ever had." In her years as a journalist, Serena had experienced many sleepless nights while covering a story, and also when David was off fighting bush fires, putting himself on the line to save others. Maggie had suffered many of those nights with her.

"Would you like me to take him?"

"He's all yours."

As Serena placed the sleeping baby in her arms, Maggie felt a rush of love as she smelled the sweet scent that all babies seemed to have. She liked to muse that it was the smell of innocence, though it was more likely due to the detergent their clothes were washed in.

"Frank said a storm's expected tonight," Serena said as she stepped down from the helicopter. She'd put on some weight during her pregnancy and was currently the heaviest she'd ever been in her life, but it looked good on her. The added weight further softened her curves and gave a pleasant round-ness to her face, filling out some of the permanent scars she carried from the blast in Paris. But what changed her appear-ance the most was the serenity Maggie noted in her eyes.

"Yes, but don't worry. We get storms all the time during the rainy season, but I'm glad you arrived before it did. Getting caught in a storm isn't fun, especially in the helicopter."

Serena laughed. "Listen to you! Don't you sound like a regular cattle station owner's wife?"

Maggie chuckled. "Well, that's what I am!"

Mother and daughter exchanged smiles and laughter as Frank and David grabbed the bags and baby paraphernalia. "I'm so glad you're here, sweetheart."

"And I'm glad to be here." Serena's expression grew serious. "How is everyone?"

Maggie exhaled a slow breath. "Doing their best. We all miss Julian. Christmas won't be the same, but we're hoping to make the best of it for everyone's sake, especially for Caleb and Sasha." Maggie felt so much for the children, who'd not only witnessed their grandmother's drowning when they were younger, but more recently, their father's car crash that resulted in his death.

Serena nodded as the two women proceeded to walk the short distance to the house. As they entered, Emma, who was sitting on the floor of the living room colouring with four-year-old Sebastian, rose to her feet and threw her arms around Serena. "I'm so glad you got here before the storm arrived. I was worried you wouldn't make it."

Serena returned her sister-in-law's hug. "Frank said we had plenty of time. The storm won't come this way for a few hours."

"I know, but storms can be unpredictable. I feel better that you're here before it starts." Being a city girl, Emma was a little nervous about spending Christmas in a place that was only accessible by air during the wet season and was also prone to flooding, although Maggie had assured her several times there was nothing to worry about.

The rest of the family gathered around David and Serena, but mostly they stood around Maggie, beaming at little Oliver.

"He's beautiful, Serena. You should be so proud." Olivia, Frank's daughter, smiled as she lifted five-year-old Isobel to look at the baby.

"He's sleeping," Isobel said. "How can I play with him if he's sleeping?"

Frank laughed from where he stood behind Maggie. "You can't play with him yet, Issie. He's too small. When he gets a bit bigger."

Isobel frowned. "Why do they always have to be so small? I don't like waiting."

"Now, Isobel, what have I told you about patience?" Frank said, lifting a brow.

Isobel didn't hesitate in her response. "A patient spirit is better than a proud spirit."

"That's right," Frank replied, smiling. The others chuckled while Olivia stepped aside so Janella could greet Serena and the baby.

The exchange between the pair was more subdued. A Christmas card had arrived the day before from one of Julian's school friends who hadn't heard the news of his passing, wishing them all a Merry Christmas and expressing hope at seeing them in the new year. The card's arrival had revived Janella's melancholy.

With the greetings over, Maggie took Serena to the guest

room that had been prepared for her, David, and baby Oliver. It was simply decorated in shades of white, pale blue, and green, with windows that opened onto the back of the house. Olivia had offered the use of William's old bassinet for Oliver now he'd outgrown it.

David and Frank left the bags in the corner of the room before returning to the living room and the rest of the family. Maggie settled Oliver into the bassinet before turning to help Serena with the unpacking.

"Are you sure you want to do this now?" she asked. They'd only just arrived and there'd be plenty of time to unpack later.

"Yes. I get so tired that if I don't do it now, it might not get done until tomorrow," Serena answered, opening one of the cases. "I'd rather be settled sooner rather than later. It'll make things easier, especially when it comes to Oliver. Routine keeps me sane. Besides, I have some meetings scheduled in town and I want to get my clothes out and have them ready."

Maggie marvelled at Serena's gusto. She had a small baby and was already gearing up for speaking engagements. Maggie should have known that she'd pursue this new career path with the same fervour she had journalism. She just didn't expect it to be so soon after Oliver's arrival.

"Couldn't David unpack?"

Serena rolled her eyes. "David's great at a lot of things but packing and unpacking is not his forté. If I left it to him, I wouldn't find anything. It's better for me to do it."

Maggie chuckled at the little idiosyncrasies that made life and marriage interesting. "Very well. At least I can help. It's faster with extra hands."

"Thanks, Mum."

The pair was halfway through the first suitcase, and Maggie was deciding on where to place Oliver's little shirts when she caught a sidelong glance from Serena. Her daughter had something to say but was hesitating. "What is it, honey?"

"Nothing." Serena shrugged, quickly busying herself with the contents of the suitcase.

Maggie stopped unpacking and studied her daughter, her eyes narrowing. "I'm not so sure about that."

Serena turned and faced her. "I was just wondering how Janella and the children are coping. It must be so hard on them, especially now it's Christmas."

Maggie nodded. "Yes, it's difficult for them. Janella puts on a brave face for the children's sake, but I can see the pain in her eyes. Caleb's taking it hard, as you'd expect. Sasha's grown quiet and stays even closer to her mother."

Serena grimaced as she lifted a blouse from the suitcase. "I can't imagine how they must feel. We've never had anyone in our family die under such tragic circumstances, and now they've had two. It seems unfair."

Maggie was silent. She wanted to tell Serena something encouraging, but she didn't have the words because she was thinking the same. It seemed unfair that the family had lost Esther, Frank's first wife, and now Julian. Why had God allowed it? Had they not prayed hard enough? She knew she should simply trust God and accept what happened as His will, but she was struggling. It seemed so unjust.

"Mum?"

Maggie snapped out of her thoughts. "Sorry. What did you say?"

"Nothing. You were just quiet. I wasn't sure if you were all right."

Maggie forced a smile. "I'm perfectly fine. Let's get this finished so we can get back to the family."

"Okay. But Mum, I want you to know that we're praying for you. Julian's death must be hard on all of you."

Hearing Serena speak so easily of prayer brought a tear to Maggie's eye. She was growing steadily in the Lord, and that made Maggie so happy. "Thank you, sweetheart. That means a lot to me, and I'm sure it will mean a lot to Frank, too."

"It's nothing, Mum. After all the prayers you've raised on my behalf, praying for you is a very little thing."

Maggie reached out her hand. "All the same, I'm grateful."

Serena turned to her with glassy eyes. Taking Maggie's hand, she stepped closer and hugged her tight. "I love you, Mum."

Maggie rubbed her daughter's back. "I love you, too, sweetheart." It was true. Having a child changed you, and Serena had certainly changed. She was softer, more caring, and more open with her feelings. Watching her bloom gave Maggie great joy.

They finished unpacking in record time, and after checking that Oliver was still asleep, the pair joined the family in the living room. Before entering, Maggie paused briefly in the doorway and took in the cosy scene. Seeing both families together like this warmed her heart so.

Other than Julian, only Stella was missing. Although she technically wasn't part of the family, Maggie had high hopes for her and Joshua. She was good for him, and despite Frank's surprise over their relationship. he was happy about it and thought highly of her, although he wasn't sure it would last.

Maggie, on the other hand, was confident it would. In fact, she sensed that Stella Martin was an answer to prayer.

She stepped into the room and joined Frank. Whatever the Lord had in store for them, beside Frank was where she belonged. She wound her arm around her husband's and patted his forearm gently as he spoke to David. Despite the sadness, they *would* have a happy Christmas.

CHAPTER 3

The following morning, Frank blinked in the dark, unfamiliar room. Where was he? Was he dreaming? No, he couldn't be. Maggie was beside him, sound asleep, and the warmth of her body was real against his.

Slowly, he remembered where they were and why. The night before, Isobel and the other children had insisted that he and Maggie stay the night so they could all be together for Christmas morning. At first, Frank wasn't sure Maggie would be willing to give up the comfort of their bed to share an old cot in the guestroom with Jeremy, Emma and the children, but to his surprise, she'd agreed almost immediately.

Raising his head, he peered around the darkened room. Only a crack of light filtered in through the blinds. They were alone. The others must have left while he and Maggie were still asleep. Which meant it was time to get up.

Reaching over, he kissed her on the cheek. "Wake up, darling. It's Christmas."

She didn't stir at first and Frank repeated the action, this time kissing her more earnestly. "Wakey. Wakey. The children will be waiting for us to open their presents." It was a Goddard family tradition to rise early on Christmas morning and gather around the tree to share and open presents before breakfast, and on the rare occasion, when they could manage it, go to church. Church wasn't an option this year with so many of them, but it didn't mean they couldn't sing Christmas hymns and pray together to celebrate Christ's birth. "Maggie?"

"I heard you," she replied huskily while stretching her arms. "How did it get to be morning so quickly? It seems like we just went to bed."

Frank laughed, brushing a salt-coloured strand of hair from her face. She was beautiful, and he was so blessed to have her as his wife. "Small children can do that to old folks like us."

Maggie's brows lifted as she pushed up on her elbows. "Speak for yourself, Frank Goddard. I am not an 'old folk.'"

"Oh? And what do you say you are?"

"Mature," she replied with a laugh, flopping back onto the pillow.

Gazing into her eyes, he gently caressed her cheek before lowering his head and brushing his lips against hers. "Good morning, my love. Merry Christmas."

Her eyes twinkled as she returned his smile. "Merry Christmas, Frank."

He could have stayed there all day with her, but the moment was broken when Isobel's excited voice sounded outside the room. "Grandpa! Wake up! It's Christmas!"

A second later, she burst through the door with Olivia on her heels.

"Isobel, no!" Olivia managed to grab her before casting an apologetic look at Frank and Maggie. "I'm sorry. I tried to stop her. She just got away from me."

"It's all right," he replied. "We were getting up anyway."

"Merry Christmas, Isobel," Maggie said. "I hope you had a good night's rest so you can open all your presents."

"I did! Now can we open them, Mummy?" She looked up at her mother with expectant eyes. "Can we? Grandpa and Grandma Maggie are up now."

"Soon, darling."

Frank and Maggie laughed together. "Grandma Maggie and I will be right out," he said before addressing Olivia. "Tell everyone we'll be right there."

Olivia nodded. "I will. I'm very sorry she disturbed you."

"It's fine, love. That's why we stayed here, so the children could wake us."

"Okay. I'll let everyone know you're coming."

Frank grinned as Olivia and Isobel left the room.

Maggie chuckled. "I think we embarrassed her."

"Do you think so?" Slipping his arms around her, Frank eased Maggie's head against the pillow and planted a kiss on her lips. "I don't know how."

"I don't know either." Laughing, she wriggled from his hold and swung her legs onto the floor. "Time to get up."

Frank nodded. She was right. They couldn't make the family wait any longer. Pushing to his feet, he stretched and slipped on his brown robe, tying the cord in a knot at his waist while Maggie headed to the bathroom down the hall.

As he followed and waited outside, the sounds of laughter echoed from the living area and brought a smile to his lips until the photo of him, Esther and their three children taken not long before she died caught his eye. The heaviness of heart that had been with him almost incessantly since Julian's passing returned.

Death was part of life, but his son had been taken too early, as had Esther. He didn't understand why, and deep down he knew he never would, at least not until his own time came and he could ask God face to face, but even then, what right did he have to question God? Whatever the reason, His ways were higher, and all Frank could do was trust Him and appreciate those around him now. Like the children. And Maggie.

As she stepped out of the bathroom, his heart swelled with gratitude. God had blessed him greatly with a second love. Not everyone got that. Smiling, he stepped towards her and kissed her gently on the top of her head. "You look lovely, my dear."

Her forehead creased with amusement. "Thank you, but I didn't do anything special. Just brushed my teeth and smoothed my hair."

"It doesn't matter. You always look beautiful."

Chuckling, she shook her head. "You're such a romantic, Frank Goddard. Come on, we'd best not keep the children waiting any longer." She linked her arm through his and together they walked down the hallway.

The entire family was in the living room. The children were seated around the pine tree that was covered in colourful ornaments of all shapes and sizes. Underneath the boughs were colourfully wrapped gifts, and at the very top, a star.

Taking in the scene, memories of many other Christmas mornings flashed through his mind. Pain stabbed his chest as his gaze settled on Janella and the children. There was no Julian this year. His son would never see another Christmas.

He licked his lips and batted away the tears that stung his eyes. This wasn't the time for tears. This was a happy day. A day to remember the goodness of God and the mercy and love He showed in sending His Son to save mankind. It wasn't a day to mourn. There had been enough of that. Today, they would rejoice. They had each other and would make the most of that. Taking a jagged breath, he smiled and shouted, "Merry Christmas, everyone!"

"Merry Christmas!" the family chorused, turning in his and Maggie's direction. There were smiles on all their faces, except one. Janella's. Frank prayed that the day and gathering of the family would bring a smile to her face, but as she sat with an arm wrapped around each of her children, there was no sign of it. *Soon, Janella. I pray your smile will return soon.*

He weaved his way across the room to his favourite chair which the others had left vacant for him. Maggie sat on his lap since all the other chairs were taken. He didn't mind in the least as she snuggled against him.

The small children opened their presents with glee. There was something for everyone. Even little Oliver had a collection of gifts waiting for him. Maggie delighted in her purchases, and as she moved to the floor to sit with the children to help open them, he couldn't help but think once more how blessed he was.

Laughter filled the room as the kids played with their toys. Frank stood and weaved his way through the bodies, toys and paper to the side buffet where he poured two glasses of juice, one for him and one for Maggie. He also grabbed a handful of the Christmas cookies Janella had made.

As he was returning to his chair, Serena called across the room. "Frank, where did you get these ornaments? I asked Mum, but she didn't know. I especially love this one with the reindeer on it."

The room instantly grew quiet.

Serena looked around, her eyes wide. "Did I say something wrong?"

"No," Frank assured her. "It's just that Julian made that ornament when he was ten. His mother liked personalising ornaments as she thought it made the season more festive. After we made them, we'd vote on whose was the best. Julian won that year."

His words dropped like stones into the suddenly silent room. Janella hugged Sasha to her side when she sniffled. Caleb hung his head. Serena looked guilty.

This wasn't what he wanted. "Has everyone had one of these cookies?" he asked, trying his best to change the solemn direction the morning had taken. "They're delectable, as usual." He smiled warmly at Janella.

"Can I get the recipe?" Emma asked. "They're so yummy, and since we can't be here every year, it'd be great to make them at home."

"Who says you can't be here every year?" Olivia asked. "All you have to do is come. The doors are always open and you're more than welcome."

The mood slowly lifted as the women continued their conversation. It wasn't long before Olivia's husband Nathan, and David, started their own discussion. Joshua stood behind

Janella and the children and whispered something to Caleb. The boy looked up with a nod before getting to his feet. A moment later, the pair was standing by the piano.

"Everyone, Caleb's going to play for us. I think a little music is just the thing to get this celebration going." Joshua smiled and patted Caleb's shoulder. "Rock it, kid."

Caleb began to play the piano, and everyone sat quietly while he played a number of traditional Christmas songs. Frank was eager to hear him, but he wasn't prepared for him to play the song Julian used to play nearly every Christmas when he was a lad.

Julian hadn't always been the serious man he'd grown into. When he was young, he was a playful and fun-loving boy who made ornaments and learned the piano under his mother's tutelage. Every year he'd amuse them in song as they sang along to their favourite Christmas carols. Then he grew up, and somewhere along the line, he began to believe that fun was no longer part of his life. He had to be serious. He had to be dependable. Amusement and music were not part of that.

It was too much. As Caleb played *The Little Drummer Boy*, tears Frank had tried to hold back would no longer be restrained. They beat angry, anguished fists against the lids of his eyes until he could no longer control them and they began trickling down his cheek.

He had to get out of there. He couldn't spoil the family's entertainment with his sorrow. Seeking refuge, he escaped to the kitchen while everyone else remained in the living room, entranced by Caleb's rendition of the beautiful carol. Gripping the edge of the counter for support, Frank's knuckles turned white as he bit back sobs. Julian was dead. His firstborn was gone.

Sobs racked his body, and in the silence of the kitchen, they were deafening. *Lord, why did You take my son? Why didn't You spare him? I know You have Your reasons, and Your thoughts and ways are higher than mine, and that there's some greater purpose to this, but I can't see it.* His sobs intensified as he slid to the floor. *I can't see it, Lord. It hurts so much.*

He gulped in air. Is this what God felt when Jesus died on the cross? Was that why He looked away because it was too much to bear? *You know how I feel, Lord. Help me endure this.*

Moments passed, and slowly, his sobs subsided.

Lord, help me find solace and joy in the midst of this sadness. Make Julian's death mean something. He left with so much undone. So much unsaid. Help me live my life to the full and cherish each second of it.

"Frank?"

He quickly wiped his face with the back of his hand before lifting his gaze. Maggie stood in the doorway, her face distraught as she hurried to him. He couldn't hide his heartache any longer. "I miss him, Maggie. I miss him so much."

She folded him into her arms. "I know, my love. I know you do." She rubbed his back and held him tight. "I miss him, too. I may not have known him that long, but I loved him. He was like a son to me."

Frank nodded. "He had his faults, but he was changing. He would have become that loving and openly affectionate person again if he'd had the time." Pulling a tissue from his pocket, he blew his nose. "I could see it happening as he worked on that old truck with Caleb." A fresh sob caught in Frank's throat as he pictured the two of them working together in the shed. "I shouldn't have let him take over the station so soon. He wasn't ready. I think that caused all the trouble between him and Joshua."

"You can't blame yourself, Frank. Julian was an adult, but regardless of his faults, everyone loved him. Including Joshua."

Frank nodded. Maggie was right. He couldn't blame himself for Julian's faults, nor for the issues between him and Joshua. Drawing a slow breath, he rose to his feet as Olivia's head appeared in the doorway.

"Dad? There you are. I'm looking for the photo album from that year when we all went to New Zealand. Do you know where it is?"

Maggie squeezed his hand, and once again, her strength allowed him to move beyond his grief. "I do," he replied, his voice brighter. "It's in the hall closet. I'll help you find it." He left Maggie and crossed the room to where Olivia stood. She meant the world to him, but he didn't say it often enough. Placing his hands on her shoulders, he looked into her eyes. "I love you, Olivia. You know that, don't you?"

Her brows scrunched as she nodded. "Yes, Dad. Of course I do."

"Good," he said softly as he slipped his arm across her shoulders. "Let's go find that album."

CHAPTER 4

$\mathcal{T}$he Hallelujah Chorus resonated in the small chapel in Cootamundra where Stella was attending Christmas morning service. She raised her hands in worship and closed her eyes as she basked in the presence of God although it saddened her that she was there on her own. Her parents were only getting out of bed when she left, having turned down the invitation to attend with her. She couldn't force them to go. She knew that, but it still saddened her.

Lord, I pray that as my family gathers today, they might be aware of the great love You showed when You sent Your Son to earth as a baby. May they see beyond the turkey and the frivolity and see You. Let this day be one of fellowship and peace as we not only enjoy each other's company, but celebrate the birth of Your Son. In Jesus' precious name. Amen.

The music faded and the congregation took their seats as the minister approached the pulpit. Although elderly, he spoke with conviction and zeal as he presented the Christmas message. Stella would never tire of hearing about God's amazing love. Of how Jesus humbled Himself and gave up everything to become a perfect sacrifice so that she, and anyone who believed, could be washed clean from sin and have the hope of eternal life with God. It was mind-blowing that He would do this when He knew that so many would reject Him.

How deep the Father's love for us,
How vast beyond all measure,
That He should give His only Son
To make a wretch His treasure.
How great the pain of searing loss –
The Father turns His face away,
As wounds which mar the Chosen One
Bring many sons to glory.

Once the service was over, Stella hurried back to help with the lunch preparations. As she opened the door of the old, weatherboard house and walked inside, the smell of roast turkey drifting down the hallway greeted her. "Mum, Dad, I'm back," she called out.

"In the kitchen," her mum replied. "Can you come and help? Your Aunt Judy was supposed to be here but she called to say she'd been held up."

Stella glanced at her watch. It was almost eleven and everyone was arriving at twelve. "I'll be right there." She rushed to her room to change. With all the family gathering for Christmas for the first time in many years, her mother was keen to make the event memorable, especially after the family had generously allowed them to move into Stella's grandmother's house when they returned to the town her mother had grown up in, penniless and jobless, after the bank foreclosed on Indigo Downs.

The house had sat vacant for many years and was in a state of disrepair, but the family agreed that if they fixed it up, they could live there at least until they became financially stable. Although much work was still needed, her parents had made it liveable.

Stella slipped out of her burgundy lace dress and into a pair of denim capris and a red and white striped blouse before rushing to the kitchen. "Where do you need me?"

"Right here," her mother replied. There was an edge to her voice and Stella sensed she was stressed. "Can you get the turkey out and baste it, and then, can you chop the last of these vegetables?"

"Sure. No worries, Mum. Is Dad carving the turkey?" Stella asked as she pulled the large bird from the oven. It was such a pity she was a vegetarian because it smelled so good, even making her stomach rumble.

"Is that your stomach, Stella?"

"Sorry, Mum. I didn't eat this morning. I didn't want to be late for church."

Her mother's gaze narrowed as she stirred a large pot of gravy. "I don't understand how you can go out without eating. What if you'd collapsed and hurt yourself?"

Stella resisted the urge to roll her eyes. Why did her mother always have to jump to the worst-case scenario? "I'm perfectly fine, Mum. Just a little hungry."

"I hope you look after yourself better while you're working. I'm sure they wouldn't want to medivac you out if you passed out because you were malnourished," her mother retorted.

Stella blinked. Medivac her out? *What was her mum talking about?* But then the penny dropped. She was still upset about losing their home and livelihood. Stella's employment at Goddard Downs was almost like rubbing the loss in her face because they'd survived while Indigo had gone under. "Mum, I have to work. And I do take care of myself, honestly. You don't have to worry about me."

Her mum stopped stirring and expelled a deep breath. "I'm sorry you had to go elsewhere to find work." She glanced at Stella over her shoulder. "I'm glad you found a job, Stell. I really am. I'd just hoped we'd be able to stay together as a family. Now we're down here and you're up there. You spent most of your childhood away from us, and now it feels like nothing has changed."

"Oh, Mum." Stella left the turkey and embraced her. "I'm sorry it happened, but you and Dad are doing so well here. You've got the teacher aide job and Dad's got the position at the council. And you've done an amazing work on this house." *Lord, let my words be encouraging.*

"Yes, we've been fortunate. I'm sorry for sounding so negative, love."

"It's okay. I know it hasn't been easy."

Her mum resumed her stirring. "Maybe it was for the best."

Stella nodded. Maybe it was. Her parents certainly seemed much happier.

By the time the rest of the family started to arrive, the cooking was complete and the tables on the back patio were set. Because her mum had been so busy preparing the food, she hadn't decorated the area, so Stella quickly put up some tinsel and placed a small, ornamental Christmas tree on the table the food would be served from. The patio had been recently painted and it looked great—much better than Stella remembered it looking when she'd visited as a youngster.

Uncle Paul, her mother's younger brother, arrived first with his wife, Aunt Janice, and their two teenage daughters, who he introduced as Christine and Lucy. Of the five Abernathy siblings, Uncle Paul and her mother looked the most alike with their straight, dark hair, hazel eyes, and tapered noses. He kissed her cheek as he entered the house, a covered dish in his hands. "Merry Christmas, Stella. You look wonderful. I can't believe how grown up you are."

"Thank you, Uncle Paul. You look well yourself. Can I take this from you?" She reached for the dish.

"Sure," he said, handing it to her. "It's the sweet potato cheese pie your Aunt Janice is known for. She wasn't sure what to make."

"It smells wonderful! I look forward to trying it."

As the two girls walked in the door behind their parents, Stella greeted them warmly, exchanging hugs as best she could with the dish in her hands. "Come in while I take this to the kitchen."

The family continued to arrive in a steady stream, the house filling to overflowing within an hour. Stella couldn't believe how many family members she had, and how few she actually knew. She had more cousins than she could count, but growing up as they had, they may as well have lived on different planets. She felt strange being with them. Those her age lived mainly in town. Some had jobs, others were unemployed. They marvelled that she was a qualified vet. Most didn't understand the draw of living off the land and herding livestock for sale. She felt out of place and missed the wide-open spaces of Goddard Downs. And Joshua.

Her father called everyone to attention with the ringing of her grandmother's bell. Stella recalled her grandmother doing the very same thing many years before on one of her family's rare treks down south to Cootamundra. Stella would only have been five or six at the time, and she thought it a fun way to gather everyone together. It was a pity her grandmother wasn't here today to see all the family gathered together.

It was a squeeze on the patio, and some of the smaller children had to sit on their parents' laps, but after everyone was settled, her father stood and waited for the noise to subside. Despite the heat of the day, he was wearing a purple sweater vest over a short-sleeved white shirt. His thinning hair was swept to one side to cover the growing bald spot, and he shuffled from one foot to the other while visibly gulping. Stella's heart went out to him. This wasn't his family—it was her mother's, and some of them hadn't been too happy when he'd whisked her away as a teenage bride and headed north to chase his dream of being a cattle baron. How humiliated he must have felt to return after losing Indigo. Yet here he was, standing before the family, about to welcome them to Christmas. A wave of pride surged through her that he could still hold his head high.

He cleared his throat before he began. "Thank you all for coming. It means the world to Gloria and me that you're here. It's a special day and although it's a tight fit out here, we're glad to see you all." He looked down at her mum and placed his hand on her shoulder. "We also want to say thank you for the welcome we received when we returned. We're grateful to have this old house to live in, and we're glad we could fix it up so we can gather together like we're doing right now. Merry Christmas, everyone. Let's dig in before the flies do."

Everyone laughed and then the older folks and those with small children went first to fill their plates. The remainder sat or stood and chatted with each other while waiting their turn. As Stella stood in the open doorway surveying the scene, a smile inched across her face. Despite missing everyone at Goddard Downs, she was glad she came.

CHAPTER 5

There was no end of surprises that day Stella discovered as her family settled into the meal and began to share stories from the past few years. There'd been marriages, divorces, and remarriages, but the standout was Aunt Claudia who'd recently married for the fourth time. Her current husband wasn't with her as he'd opted to spend Christmas skiing the slopes in Switzerland with his teenage daughter from his second marriage. Although her aunt didn't seem bothered, Stella wondered if the marriage would last.

As one of her cousins told the story of how Aunt Claudia met her current husband when she was stuck with him in an elevator for three hours, Stella tried to hide her grin behind a spoonful of pavlova, but her aunt caught her. "And what are you grinning about, Stella? We've heard from almost everyone at the table but you. Anyone special in your life?"

All gazes swung to her and she momentarily froze. Was she prepared to share her new relationship with them? What she and Joshua felt for each other seemed too precious to talk about, at least not yet, and not with people she didn't really know, even if they were family. But how could she in all honesty say there wasn't anyone special?

Smiling, she shook her head and prayed that God and Joshua would forgive her. "Not really."

"I don't believe that for a second. That grin meant something. You just don't want to share," her aunt challenged with a laugh. "All right. Have your secrets. I had plenty of them when I was your age."

Stella said nothing but turned in her parents' direction. Her father was focused on his bowl of pavlova, but her mother was looking at her thoughtfully. Stella smiled and her mother smiled back as the conversations continued.

By the time the stars were out, Stella felt at home amidst her family. She got to know her cousins better, and despite their differences, they found some common ground in movies, books, and music. Sadly, it seemed that none of her family shared her beliefs, although she couldn't be sure of that without talking with them all. Even then, she knew that people often weren't comfortable talking about what they believed, especially with someone they didn't know. It was far easier to stick with less contentious topics. However, on the surface, it appeared she was on her own.

Her own faith had come via her paternal grandmother whom she'd lived with on and off for years while Stella was sick. She sometimes wondered what had made her father walk away from faith when his own mother was such a devout believer, but she had hope that one day he'd return.

Fix these words of Mine in your hearts and minds; tie them as

symbols on your hands and bind them on your foreheads. Teach them
to your children, talking about them when you sit at home and when
you walk along the road, when you lie down and when you get up.

It seemed that no one had taught her mother's family about
God. From the little she'd said, Stella gleaned that her mother's
early childhood was riddled with abuse and poverty. Her
grandfather was a drunk who beat her grandmother for no
reason at all, and since he was unable to keep a job, the family
struggled to make ends meet. Her grandmother, however, did
what she could to ensure the children never went hungry and
did her best to protect them from their abusive father.

After Stella's grandfather passed away from cirrhosis of the
liver in his early forties, her grandmother devoted herself to
giving her five children the best life possible. Stella's mum was
ten when he died. Her grandmother, whose house they were
now in, passed away six years ago at the age of seventy-three.

Looking at the extended family, Stella was sure her grandmother would be proud at how they'd all turned out. They
were good people. They just didn't know God.

She prayed once more that while they were celebrating
Christmas, her parents in particular might appreciate the real
meaning of the holiday and open their hearts to Him. That
would be the best Christmas present ever.

THE HOUSE WAS FINALLY QUIET. Midnight was almost upon
them, and Stella and her mother were in the kitchen washing
dishes. Her father was outside tidying the patio.

While Stella scraped leftovers into the bin, she glanced at

her mum who was elbows deep in suds. "I enjoyed seeing everyone today," she said.

"Yes, it was a wonderful day. I'm already looking forward to doing it again next year."

"Really? You think you'll stay here?"

"Yes." Her mum stopped washing and turned around, a gleam on her face. "This is the happiest we've been in a long time. I'm sure you saw what the stress of running Indigo was doing to Dad."

Stella nodded. It was slowly destroying him.

"It put our marriage under pressure, and then I was angry at him for losing the station, but since we've been here and we haven't had that weight pressing down on us, things have turned around and we're happy again."

The shimmer in her mother's eyes pushed Stella forward. She wrapped her arms around her in a long hug. "I'm so glad for you, Mum. For you and Dad."

"Thank you, sweetheart." Her mother's voice faltered as she patted Stella gently on the back. "We got to start over, love. Not every couple gets that chance."

Stella laughed to herself. She'd been so determined to get Indigo back for her parents, but God already had a plan for them. They were doing so much better than they had at Indigo. If she'd succeeded in getting it back, she would have only caused them more stress and worry. *Thank You, Lord. Thank You for knowing better than me, and for doing exactly what You needed to do. I pray that this change will open my parents' hearts to You and to Your love. That they'll see this as You at work in their lives, and not simply as a random set of events.*

"And what about you, Stella?"

She released her mother and stepped back. "Me?"

"Yes, what about you? How are you adjusting to the change of being somewhere else? Of letting go of Indigo. I know you were upset when we lost it."

She leaned back against the counter and folded her arms. "As you said, I had to let go." She smiled wistfully. "It was for the best."

Nodding, her mother returned to the dishes. "Running a station is difficult these days. At least you were able to find a job. It's just a pity it's so far away."

"I couldn't have asked for a better position, Mum. The Goddards have accepted me, and I feel like part of their family. Frank, Maggie, Olivia and Nathan, Janella, and the children. Joshua."

Her cheeks warmed at the mention of his name, and again, she found herself smiling.

Her mother glanced her way, a lopsided grin on her face. "There it is."

"What?"

"What your aunt was saying at lunch. That smile. I see it now. So there *is* someone special."

Stella's hands dropped to her sides. "Is it that obvious?"

Her mother chuckled. "A little."

A groan, mingled with a laugh, escaped from Stella as she shifted her weight from one leg to the other. "I didn't want to say anything."

Her mother left the dishes and turned around. "So, who is he?"

Stella held her mother's gaze, her stomach flipping like she was a teenager again. "Joshua Goddard."

"Frank's youngest?"

Stella nodded. "We've been seeing each other for four months. Ever since his brother passed away."

Her mother's lips twisted in sympathy. "I'm so sorry for them. I can only imagine how difficult that must have been for Frank and the family after losing Esther a few years ago. It's so very sad."

"It was. It is."

Her mum returned to the dishes while Stella waited for her to say something about her announcement. She assumed she'd be happy, relieved even, to hear she was dating, although she might not be too happy to hear it was Joshua Goddard.

"Is it serious?" she finally asked. Because she didn't look around, Stella was unable to tell from her facial expression what her thoughts were, but her tone was ominously neutral.

Stella's lips parted but nothing came out. *Was it serious?* She thought of Joshua constantly. She looked forward to seeing him every day. They seemed to fit in a way she never had with anyone before. Yet, did that make it serious? What qualified a relationship as serious? Time? Understanding? She wasn't sure. Besides, she didn't know if Joshua's feelings ran that deep. He was still dealing with Julian's death. She hardly thought he was considering the depth of his feelings for her at this point. "We're taking it slowly."

Her mother nodded. "Good. He's grieving. That makes a person vulnerable to making decisions they might not make if they were thinking rationally."

Stella bristled. What was her mother suggesting? "Are you saying that Joshua is dating me out of some kind of coping mechanism?"

Her mother faced her. "I wasn't saying that. I'm sorry if you took it that way. I'm sure that if Joshua chose to date you it was because he has true feelings for you, not because he's using you to make himself feel better. I didn't mean for it to come out that way. Forgive me?"

Stella nodded. Joshua didn't want her in his life to fill the hole Julian's death had made. She believed that. He'd wanted more between them long before she agreed to a relationship. Since Alice Springs, he'd wanted to date her but she'd refused. Still, something inside her wondered. Could there be some truth to what her mother said?

"What do you feel for him?"

The comforting voice and her mother's question distracted her from the earlier remark. How *did* she feel about Joshua? "I like him very much."

"Just *like*?" Her mother's brow lifted as bubbles from the tub rose before her face.

Stella chuckled. "I more than like him," she admitted, as longing filled her heart. "I feel very deeply for him, Mum. More than I've ever felt for anyone else."

"Is that so?"

"Yes. He's not perfect by any degree, but the more we get to know each other, and the more I learn about him, the more perfect he seems to be for me. Is that crazy?"

Her mother chortled. "Not at all. Sometimes you just know."

"Know what?" Stella's stomach began to knot. This wasn't the conversation she'd intended to have, but they were having it. She only hoped she wasn't setting herself up for disappointment. That she wasn't reading more into the relationship than there was. More than Joshua was able to give.

"The right person for you. I knew it with your father, and despite our ups and downs, I wouldn't want to be sharing my life with anyone else."

Stella's heart jumped inside her chest. Was she in love with Joshua in the way her parents loved each other? The forever kind of love? Was she ready for that type of commitment? *Was Joshua?*

She remained thoughtful as she packed up the rest of the food. She thought she'd learn something from talking to her mother, but instead, she'd ended up with more questions.

CHAPTER 6

Frank knew that Christmas would be challenging. He knew there'd be sadness over Julian's death, but never did he imagine the degree of pain his son's absence would have on *him*.

His heart ached through the morning and the opening of the presents. It ached through the saying of grace and lunch. Last year, Julian had said it. It ached as they sat that night and he read the Bible to everyone, recounting the story of the Saviour's birth. Now, days later, it still ached, but listening to the gentle timbre of Maggie's breaths as she slept with her head on his shoulder, he remembered that there was a season for everything. *There is a time for everything, and a season for every activity under the heavens. A time to be born and a time to die. A time to plant and a time to uproot. A time to kill and a time to heal.*

A time to heal. When would that time arrive? When would the aching stop? When would the tears stop flowing? When would the memories of his son stop eliciting more pain than joy? *I should have done better by Julian. I should have done more to stop my sons from squabbling. Perhaps none of this would have happened if I'd listened more. Joshua mightn't have been as unsettled, and Julian might still be alive.*

Frank took a deep breath while gently rubbing Maggie's arm. What would happen now? He'd already accepted that he'd have to take back responsibility for the station, at least until Joshua showed signs of wanting to run it, although Frank had doubts that would ever happen. He lowered his gaze to Maggie's sleeping form. They'd have to put their travel plans on hold. She wouldn't like it, but she'd be good about it. It was her nature. She understood things, and he was glad of that. Some wives wouldn't understand.

His fingers found themselves entangled in the silken tresses of her hair before he kissed her on the forehead. She didn't stir, not that he wanted her to. He was enjoying the silence and that steady rhythm of her breathing. However, her serenity wasn't to last. A few minutes later, the firm knock of a strong hand against their front door woke her and set Frank on his feet. Who could it be at this hour? He checked the clock to make sure his watch was right. It was not yet six a.m.

"Who is it, Frank?" Maggie asked in a groggy voice, wiping the sleep from her eyes before raising her arms above her head to stretch.

Frank looked at her and shrugged. "I don't know. I'll go check."

He headed to the door, and pulling back the curtain, peeked out the window. Joshua stood outside in the pale light of early morning, head down and hands stuffed deep into the pockets of his jeans.

Frank called back. "It's Joshua." He turned the lock and opened the door. "Good morning, son. What brings you here this time of day?"

"I know it's early, but can I come in?"

"Sure." Frank's brows came together as he stepped aside to let Joshua pass. "Is something wrong?"

"Not really. I just couldn't sleep." Joshua headed for the living room where Maggie now sat on the couch, wrapped in her robe. Frank followed, a twinge of concern gnawing at his gut. It was never a good thing when people came by at such an hour. Surely there was no more bad news to be had, but still, he steeled himself.

"Good morning, Maggie." Joshua tipped his hat before removing it and placing it on the side table. "I'm sorry to stop by so early, but I needed to talk to Dad."

"It's fine, Joshua. I'm sure you wouldn't be here if it wasn't important. I'll leave the two of you alone," she replied, getting to her feet.

"You can stay. It might be good for you to hear this as well. You could help."

Frank eyes widened. *Joshua wanted to talk and was willing to allow Maggie in on the conversation?* That was a first. Even more curious was the fact that he was asking for help. His son, who did everything on his own and marched to his singular drum, was coming to them for help. Frank groaned. He had to be in trouble. Why else would he come asking for help? "If that's the case, let's all sit down."

Frank sat beside Maggie while Joshua pulled one of the single chairs closer to the couch. Frank remained silent as his son leaned over, resting his elbows on his knees, his hands folded together. Frank tried to ignore the thundering of his heart as he imagined the worst.

Maggie, as if sensing his distress, took hold of his hand and squeezed it gently. She said she'd go through anything with him. Frank was sure that her words were about to be put to the test.

"Dad. Maggie. I have something I need to say to you. I don't know how you'll take it, or if you'll approve, but I've made a decision and I want you to be the first to know."

Frank's brow knitted. "A decision?"

"Yes. A decision about my future," Joshua replied, his hands locked together so tightly his knuckles were white.

Frank exchanged a glance with Maggie before he swung his gaze back to Joshua. Perhaps he wasn't in trouble after all—maybe he was simply planning on leaving. If that was the case, they'd deal with it. It would mean Frank and Maggie would be tied to the station a lot longer than expected since he didn't trust non-family members to run the business, but they'd manage. His gaze held firmly as he asked, "What have you decided, son?"

Joshua's Adam's apple bobbed as he spoke. He looked downright uncomfortable. "You know that Stella and I have been seeing each other these past months."

Frank nodded, his eyes narrowing.

Joshua moved forward in his seat. "What you don't know is how serious I am about her. With everything that's happened, I realise how short life is, and how precious. I don't want to waste it, Dad. I feel as if I've wasted so much already, and I don't want to do that anymore. I want to choose what happens next, not wait for it to sneak up on me."

Frank's brow furrowed further. "What are you saying, son?"

Joshua straightened, his jaw firming. "I'm saying that I want to marry her. I love her, and I know she loves me. I don't want to waste any more time when I already know what I want."

Maggie gasped, but Frank was too stunned to speak. Marriage? He searched the depths of his son's gaze and found determination staring back at him. His son had come prepared for opposition and looked ready to defend himself. But he didn't need to. Frank wouldn't fight him. Not this time. "Marriage is a great commitment, son. Are you certain this is what you want?"

"Yes, Dad. I know you think I'm too irresponsible, but Julian's death changed me."

"I just want to be sure you've thought this through."

"I have."

Their gazes remained locked until Frank reached out and shook Joshua's hand. "Then I'm happy for you."

Joshua blinked as Maggie laughed and congratulated him. "You've made a wonderful choice. Stella's a great girl."

"She is," Frank agreed. "She's been an asset to this place since the day she began. She's filled the vet's shoes better than anyone could have imagined. I'm happy with her work and would be happy to see her added to the family."

Leaning back, Joshua dispelled a long breath. "I'm so relieved. I thought you'd try to stop me since we haven't been dating long."

Frank shook his head. "Why would I do that? You're a grown man, Joshua. You can make decisions for yourself. You don't need me to approve."

If Frank wasn't mistaken, Joshua's eyes misted over. He

quickly swiped them with the back of his hand, as if embarrassed. "You really mean that?"

"Of course. I trust you, Joshua. I may not have always said it, but I do. I'm sorry if I didn't tell you enough or if I made you feel I didn't trust you. I never meant to." The words slipped unbidden from his lips. He was sorry for many things, but at least God was giving him the chance to correct some of them. Perhaps this would be the start of the healing process between him and his son.

Joshua's voice cracked as he said, "Thanks, Dad. That means a lot."

Maggie squeezed Frank's arm and smiled brightly. "This is wonderful news, Joshua. Goddard Downs needs something to celebrate."

"Yes, I agree," Frank said. "When do you plan on telling the others?"

Joshua raked his fingers through his dark hair. "As soon as I ask Stella."

The three laughed together. "That would be a good idea," Frank said. "Does she know how deeply you feel?"

"I think so. I hope so. I want to propose when she gets back from Cootamundra. I just need to buy a ring."

"Picking an engagement ring is a big deal. Do you have anything in mind?" Frank asked.

"Not really. I don't know much about these things," Joshua admitted.

"Then why don't you let Maggie help you with that?" Frank took her hand and patted it. "I'm sure she can help you find the perfect ring for Stella."

Maggie's eyes widened and Frank gulped. "I should have

asked first, love, but you'd be willing to help Joshua out, wouldn't you?"

Joshua leaned forward. "You don't have to if it's too much trouble, but I'd greatly appreciate it if you could."

She diffused the tension with a smile. "Of course, I will, Joshua. I'd be pleased to help, and it'll give us a chance to spend some time together. I'll look forward to that."

Relief washed over his face. "Thank you."

Frank sat quietly watching the exchange between his wife and son. This was a good thing, an opportunity for the pair to get to know each other better. Of all the members of his family, Joshua interacted with Maggie the least. Frank wasn't sure if it had to do with his busy schedule or whether there was something more. Whatever the reason, they now had a chance to spend some time together and see if there wasn't more that connected them besides him. He still wasn't sure whether this was the start of their time to heal, or if he was rushing it, but Frank wanted Joshua to settle. If Stella was the person to lead him towards that, then he'd welcome her happily into the family.

"I should probably get going since I've got a busy day," Joshua said as he pushed to his feet.

Maggie stood beside him. "Let me know when you want to go ring hunting."

He nodded. "Perhaps later this week?"

"Sounds fine to me," she replied.

"Then it's a date." Joshua grinned and headed to the door.

After he left, Maggie slipped her arms around Frank's waist and gazed up at him. "That was a surprise."

He chuckled. "You can say that again."

That evening, as the two of them settled in for a cup of tea and Sasha's freshly baked cookies after dinner, he still couldn't believe Joshua's news. He bit into the cookie, its crispy edge giving way to a moist, chewy centre. His granddaughter had her mother's talents in the kitchen, though in a different vein. While Janella was a master at cooking, Sasha was proving herself to be quite a baker. Since her father's death, she'd spent more and more time in the kitchen beside her mother, and each time, she created something delectable.

"I'm sure I've gained a few pounds from Sasha's baking," Frank commented as he sank his teeth into another cookie.

"Whether you did or not, it doesn't really matter." Maggie groaned as she took another bite herself. "These are so good."

Frank agreed with a hum, his mouth too full to respond. He settled back in his seat and followed up the morsel with a sip of tea.

"How are you feeling?" Maggie asked quietly.

He turned to her. He knew what she meant, and like the amazing woman she was, she knew that his mind was still reeling without him having to say so. "I'm not sure."

"It was a bit of a shock. I know I was surprised."

"It was. But if Joshua's happy, then I'm happy."

Maggie studied him closely, her gaze narrowing. "Are you?"

Frank expelled a heavy breath. "I truly am. There's no denying that he's made his share of mistakes. We all have. I can't keep holding those mistakes against him. I need to give him space and trust him like I said. I think I've treated him like a child for too long."

"You don't think he's rushing it?"

Frank gave a small shrug. "Maybe. It's only been four

months since Stella arrived, but in that time she's proven herself to be level-headed and dependable. Not to mention, she loves the Lord, and since she's been in his life, Joshua's had more of an inclination towards God than he has since his mother's death. I think that says something."

Maggie nodded. "She's a very good influence on him."

"That she is." Frank expelled another long breath. "I think for the first time I understand where Joshua is right now. He's realised that nothing's guaranteed and he doesn't want to waste the chances he gets. I felt the same when you and I met." He leaned over and planted a kiss on the side of her head. "How can I not support him?"

Maggie snuggled against him. "I hope they'll be happy together. I just hope Stella says yes."

Frank blinked. He hadn't thought of that. What if Stella didn't share Joshua's feelings? Had his son thought of that? A sudden pain pierced his chest. He rubbed the left side hoping to dispel it.

"Are you okay, Frank?" Maggie lifted her head, her face etched with worry.

"A little heartburn, I think."

She frowned. "You did have two helpings of that curry, and it was very spicy. I'll get some baking soda water."

She stood, and despite the pain, Frank grabbed her hand.

Her face pinched with concern. "What's the matter, Frank?"

"Nothing. I just wanted to tell you how much I love you."

She chuckled. "I love you, too, but let me get that baking soda water. And what about another pot of tea? Perhaps chamomile this time."

Frank grinned and set his mug aside. "That sounds

wonderful. I think I might have overdone the decadence for one day."

"Perhaps we both did." She gave another small chuckle as she headed for the kitchen. "I'll be right back."

"Good. I'm not going anywhere."

CHAPTER 7

aggie's hands were clammy as she dressed to meet Joshua for their trip to Kununurra. It was the first time she and her stepson would be alone together, and although it was a chance to get to know one another, which Maggie wanted, she was also a little anxious.

Following her divorce, she didn't expect to remarry, let alone consider she'd ever become a stepmother, yet here she was, married to the most wonderful man and a stepmother to three. She quickly corrected herself. Stepmother to two, now that Julian was gone. Not that she could ever take Esther's place. She didn't want to. But being married to their father meant she was a part of the family.

While Olivia and Janella had welcomed her and made her feel she belonged, the boys had never really taken to her. In fact, she was sure that at times her presence was resented. She could still remember the look on Julian's face when she tried to intercede in his argument with Joshua.

Joshua was a different matter altogether. Other than his spats with Julian, he rarely showed emotion, therefore, she had no idea what he was thinking. Despite what he'd said, she wasn't sure that he truly wanted her to go with him that day and had agreed simply to please his father.

Lord, help me today. Bless this outing and help Joshua and me to find a middle ground, to accept one another in whatever capacity. He may not see me as a mother figure, but I pray he'll allow me to be his friend. We all need each other following Julian's death. As we try to move forward and rebuild, I pray that You'll be with us and that You'll give us peace amidst our sorrow. Help us to be there for each other. In Jesus' precious name. Amen.

She tugged in her earrings to pull the hoops into their proper place before leaving the bedroom. Frank was already gone since he had an early morning call with Ravi Tamala. The negotiations were proceeding well and Maggie expected that very soon things would be settled and the station would be supplying the extra beef to Ravi's enterprise. In the meantime, discussions were being held amongst the family to ensure everyone was comfortable with the arrangements, and when necessary, adjustments were made. However, the main issue was still figuring out how they could accommodate a larger herd without sacrificing quality. They could easily run more cattle, but Frank in particular was concerned they'd be compromising the quality if they did. They were all praying for a solution.

Maggie grabbed her keys and put them in her purse. Joshua was picking her up at ten and it was nearly that time. She walked into the living room and reached the front door just as she heard a knock. She peeked through the curtain before opening the door. She smiled. "Good morning, Joshua."

"Good morning, Maggie. You look lovely today."

"Thank you. And you look very handsome." She took in the way his pale blue shirt hugged the muscles in his arms. The sleeves were buttoned at the wrist for a change, instead of rolled up to his elbows. That wasn't the only difference. He was wearing tan trousers instead of his customary jeans, and if she wasn't mistaken, she detected a hint of cologne. He was going all out to buy an engagement ring.

He looked over his attire. "You don't think it's too much? I wanted to make a good impression."

Her head tilted. "On whom?" She had no idea who he'd need to impress other than Stella, who as far as Maggie knew, was still in Cootamundra. "Stella's not back, is she?"

"No," Joshua replied with a shake of his head. "I want the salespeople to see a man who is ready for marriage. Someone who should be in their store to buy an engagement ring."

Maggie smiled. "I think you fit that bill no matter what you wear."

"You're too kind. I just felt that," he shrugged, "I don't know...that I need to present a good face," he said with a chuckle. "I guess I'm being silly."

"Not at all. This is a very important moment. You want everything to go perfectly."

He nodded solemnly. "I want to be the man Stella deserves."

Maggie placed a comforting hand on his arm. "You are. She wouldn't be with you if you weren't. Come on, let's get to Kununurra. You have a ring to buy."

The flight to town was uneventful, although Maggie never tired of seeing the countryside from the air. Awe filled her as she gazed across the vast savannah plains and the rivers that had burst their banks and spread so much they looked like inland lakes.

Situated amidst the picturesque hills and ranges of the north-east Kimberley region, Kununurra was a town formed to service the Ord River Irrigation Scheme and was the largest town in the region. Mostly made up of outlying farmland, it was hard to believe that the rugged ochre outcrops lay beyond the lush green fields of mangoes, melons, and sugar cane. It seemed like two vastly different places as they flew overhead and eventually landed at the helipad.

They picked up a taxi and travelled into the town centre where most shops and restaurants were located. They'd done their homework before travelling, picking a few stores to visit that were in close proximity to save time.

The first store they went to was promising. They had a variety of stones and cuts, all of which were stunning, but far too expensive for what they were offering. Maggie understood the concept of supply and demand, but they were a bit ridiculous with their pricing, and after only a few minutes of looking around, she urged Joshua to look elsewhere.

The second store, a swanky little place where they had to buzz you in to enter, was better in price but smaller on selection. The pieces were very nice, but both Maggie and Joshua felt that there was better elsewhere.

The third store was the winner. The sales representative was pleasant and immediately greeted them when they entered. She was a young woman, no more than thirty, and her eyes lit up the second she spotted Joshua. Whether he realised it or not, Joshua Goddard was a handsome man and reminded Maggie of Frank in appearance.

"How may I help you today?" the young woman asked. The tag on her blouse said her name was Amy.

"Good day, Amy. We're looking for an engagement ring."

The young woman looked at them curiously. "An engagement ring?"

It was then Maggie realised the young woman's confusion. Chuckling, she answered, "It isn't for me if that's what you're thinking."

"I didn't think anything," Amy replied.

"No, the ring isn't for Maggie. She's my stepmother," Joshua stated. It was the first time Maggie had heard him say the word aloud and it made her smile.

"Very well. Do you have any idea what kind of ring you're looking for?" Amy asked.

Joshua shook his head. "Show me what you have and I'll figure it out."

Amy led them to a showcase filled with rings. They were gold, platinum, and rose in colour, with gems that sparkled under the strategically placed lighting. The rings were stunning and were more affordable than what they'd seen earlier.

Joshua hovered over the case as Maggie stood beside him observing. There were so many to choose from that she imagined it was difficult to pick one, but Joshua had such focus that it made her heart light. He was very serious about Stella. It showed in the way he wanted to ensure she had the right ring.

"That one."

Amy pulled a large princess cut diamond ring from the

display and held it out to him. Maggie had never seen such a large stone, and her eyes widened when she saw the price tag. "That one, Joshua? Are you sure?"

"Yes. Don't you like it?" He turned to her and placed the ring in her hand for her to look at.

"It's stunning," Maggie replied, her mouth twisting slightly as she considered it.

"What's wrong?"

"Nothing."

He looked at her keenly. "Please, Maggie. What is it? I know you're thinking something. Why don't you just say it?"

She lifted her gaze from the ring and placed it back in his hand. "It just doesn't seem to be Stella."

He frowned. "What do you mean?"

"It doesn't seem like something she would wear," Maggie explained.

His forehead creased and his shoulders drooped. "What's wrong with it? Isn't it big enough?"

"It's more than big enough. It's just not what I picture Stella wearing."

"I thought women always wanted a big stone."

Maggie smiled at her stepson's naivety. "No, Joshua. That isn't all a woman wants. In fact, a woman doesn't want a big stone just for the sake of having it. She wants something that proves you know who she truly is. She wants something that reflects her and shows that you put thought into what she likes. That you know her tastes." She shifted closer and looked at the ring in his hand. "When you look at that, does it say, 'Stella' to you?"

He studied the piece for no more than a second before replying, "No. It doesn't."

"Then it isn't for her."

He handed the ring back to Amy and started looking again. This time he took longer, carefully perusing each line of rings. He asked for several before he finally settled on one. This one was simpler, more classic in appearance, with a solitaire diamond and twisted rope band in white gold. He held it up to the light. "This is the one."

Maggie smiled. "Are you sure?"

"Definitely. This is Stella. It's simple, uncomplicated, but wraps you up completely, just the way she did to me," Joshua said, grinning. "I think she'll really like this one. What do you think, Maggie?"

"I think it's perfect."

His grin broadened as he gave the ring back to Amy and asked her to wrap it. He turned back to Maggie. "That took less time than I expected."

"It did. I was sure we'd be here for a couple of hours at least," she replied. "What do you want to do now? Head back to the helipad?"

"No. I think we should celebrate finding a ring so quickly. What do you say to lunch on me?" The cheer in his voice echoed the joy in his heart. In the two years she'd been part of the family, she'd never seen him so happy.

"I think lunch sounds wonderful."

"Great. Let me pay for the ring and I'll take you to this nice little place Stella introduced me to. It has some of the best juices around, and the chef uses only farm to table produce, nothing frozen or preserved. It makes the food that much better."

Maggie chuckled. "I had no idea things like that interested you."

"They do. I care about what I put in my body, though you might not think so. I know this is the only one I have and I need to take care of it. Besides, I can't afford to get sick with all the work we have to do. But to be honest, I mostly like it because of Stella. Everything she does is carefully thought out." He grinned. "Everything except dating me."

"I'd say that was a good choice." Maggie gave him a wink.

Amy returned with the ring in a bag and placed the sales invoice in front of Joshua. He pulled out his card for her to swipe. Once the ring was paid for, he and Maggie left the store and strolled towards the restaurant he had mentioned.

"Thank you for saying that," he stated as they crossed the street.

"Saying what?"

"For saying that Stella dating me is a good choice. It means a lot."

"I think very highly of you, Joshua. I'm very glad for you and Stella. I wish you the very best."

"Thank you." He stopped walking and looked at her intently. "Thanks for coming with me today. I know we haven't always gotten along. We've hardly spoken since you married Dad, and I'm sorry about that. I guess I was a little upset about it at first."

Maggie nodded. "I suspected as much."

"I'm sorry. I should have given you a chance before now." He paused and held her gaze. "How about we start over?"

"I'd like that," Maggie answered, blinking back tears. "How about we start with a hug?"

He smiled and stepped towards her. "Thanks for being part of the family, Maggie. I'm glad Dad married you."

Warmth filled her as Joshua wrapped his arms around her. It felt wonderful, as though they were truly starting afresh. God had certainly answered her prayers this time.

CHAPTER 8

*D*ark clouds blanketed the sky as the sun fought a losing battle to maintain dominance. Though the heaviness of the coming showers loomed in the air, no rain fell as Joshua leaned against the helicopter, his arms folded over his chest, waiting for Stella to arrive. He checked his watch. She was late. He tapped his foot; he was as nervous as a jackrabbit and just as excited.

He had his father's approval and the ring. Now all he needed was to ask Stella to marry him. *And for her to say yes.* He had a plan and just hoped it would come off.

His proposal might come as a surprise, but he had every hope she would say yes. He loved her, and he was sure she loved him. Others may think it too soon, but he didn't care. He hoped Stella wouldn't either. He knew what he wanted, and that was to be with her for the rest of his life. She'd shown strength in refusing his advances until he'd gotten himself in the right place. He hadn't been ready for a serious relationship before meeting her, and if she'd said yes two years ago, they probably wouldn't be where they were now. *Everything has its right time.*

His heart quickened as a taxi pulled up. He leaned to one side, eager to see if Stella was inside. She was. His heart doubled its pace as he forced himself to stand upright. He brushed the front of his shirt, the fabric making a swishing sound under his hand as he brushed away imaginary dust.

He strode towards her. With every step, the smile on his face grew. He was happy to see a large grin on her face as well. Wearing a light rain poncho that came all the way to her ankles, her clothing was hidden except for the hems of her jeans peeking out. She wore a fedora on her head that was once tan, but with the rain, it was now a dark brown. She looked positively drenched, and yet she was still the most beautiful woman Joshua had ever seen. "Got caught in the rain, I see." Not caring how damp she was, he wrapped her in his arms. Oh, it felt good to be holding her again. He kissed the side of her damp hair. "I've missed you so much, Stella."

"And I've missed you, Josh. It's great to be home." She pulled back and gave him the most gorgeous of smiles, one that made him think of sunshine and daisies.

He cupped her cheeks and kissed her passionately. He would have been happy to stay and kiss her all day, but the rain could catch them at any moment. They needed to get going.

He took her bag and they headed to the helicopter.

"The taxi was late, and the sky just opened up. I barely had a chance to get my poncho on before the downpour started. The joys of living in the north."

He could listen to her chatter forever. "I have some towels

in the chopper. You can dry off a bit before we get home. You should probably change clothes, but from the look of the sky, I doubt we have much time before the rain reaches us. We should get going."

Stella shrugged. "I'll be fine."

There was another reason why he wanted them to leave right away. He intended to fly over Indigo so she could see her childhood home, then, when she was happy and lost in her memories, he planned to pull out the ring and propose. It sounded like a good plan to him. He hoped she'd think so too.

He stuffed her bag in the back while she got into the co-pilot's seat. He reached into his bag and stuffed the box containing the ring into his pocket. He walked around the front of the helicopter and climbed in. Starting the engine, he looked at her and smiled. "Here we go."

She removed her hat and shook her hair out. The golden strands were now dark, clumping together around her shoulders and frizzing where it was dry.

"Did I tell you how beautiful you look?"

"No, you didn't, but I hardly think I deserve the compliment right now."

"What are you talking about? You look great." *Better than great. Gorgeous.*

She laughed heartily. "You're just saying that. I look like a drowned wallaroo. Hardly a beauty."

He chuckled. "Then you're the prettiest wallaroo in all of Australia."

"Thank you, Joshua." She said his name with a smile as a blush crept up her cheeks. He gazed at her, thankful that the helicopter didn't require as keen a focus as a car because all he wanted to do was gaze at her. Drink her in. He admired her hair, fighting the urge to coil the strands around his fingers and inhale the lavender scent. He didn't know what shampoo she used, but the scent was unmistakable. He loved it. It didn't seem possible, but she looked better than when she'd left.

"Did things go well with your family?" he asked as Kununurra grew smaller beneath them.

"Better than I imagined. It was good getting to know my family, especially the ones I'd not met before. It was also wonderful seeing how well my parents are doing. You know, I thought they'd still be upset about losing the station, but they're actually happier now than they've ever been."

"Really?" Joshua's brow lifted.

"Yes. Mum's enjoying her teacher aide position and Dad's happy with his job in the council. The reduced responsibility and stress mean he can take it easier. He looks younger, if you can believe that."

Joshua smiled. "That's good. I'm sure that made you happy."

"It did. It also made me see how foolish I've been about Indigo." She flopped back against her seat. "I wanted to get it back for them, but they didn't need it. They're doing fine all by themselves."

Joshua turned as Stella spoke. Her head was down and her voice was quiet. Despite what she said, he could tell she still missed her home on the station. Getting it back had meant so much to her. He nodded to himself. His plan *should* work. He turned the helicopter in the direction of Indigo.

Stella was distracted by drying her hair and seemingly didn't notice their change of direction. Joshua grinned as the arid, harsh lands appeared, leaving all traces of the town behind. It took several minutes before the wild land changed into something more ordered. There were stations and farms all around Kununurra, but the trail to Indigo was uninhabited and isolated.

She flipped her hair forward, drying the back strands as she hummed a tune. Stella loved singing; it was something Joshua had noticed long before they became a couple. It was as if she was always happy, even when she wasn't. She had joy in her heart, just like that song they used to sing in Sunday school as children.

Indigo Downs was one hundred and twenty kilometres south of Kununurra. The landscape changed less than ten minutes after leaving the town, and soon, they were flying over the familiar setting of a cattle station.

Joshua wasn't sure when Stella realised where they were, but when he faced her, her eyes were wide and her mouth agape as she stared at the station below. Her eyes lit up and a broad smile filled her face with joy. She whispered softly, "Indigo."

He took in the station, noting the various buildings. He could make out the homestead beneath them, what looked like a mechanic shop off to the right, and a plant nursery nearby. The high ground was sandy brown and pale red, with splatters of brown and pale green grass, and the occasional large cluster of bright green from the trees. It reminded him of a quilt. In the distance, where the land was greenest, there was a large body of water.

"Is that a lake?"

"A dam," Stella replied. "It's part of the irrigation system. I wanted to use it for hydropower."

"That's a brilliant idea. Why didn't you?"

"It costs a lot to do the conversion and the money never presented itself. I prayed so much for some way to make it happen, but it never did. I suppose it was God's way of telling me not to waste my money since the station wasn't going to stay in the family, anyway."

His heart ached for her. He couldn't imagine what his family would do if they lost Goddard Downs. It would never happen as long as he lived. His father would never allow it, but neither would he. He loved the station, even if at one time he'd wanted to go his own way. He reached out and took her hand. "I'm so sorry you lost it, Stella."

Melancholy tainted the beautiful cadence of her voice. "Thank you. I had such wonderful times here. After being in the hospital for so long, and being away from my parents because of it, finally living at Indigo was like a dream. I was determined never to leave. I wanted to spend the rest of my life on the station. I was sure it would happen. It was all I thought of."

She took a long breath as Joshua brought the helicopter to a hover over the homestead. It was a bungalow, not unlike Goddard Downs, although it was about half the size. It did house fewer people; there'd been only Stella and her parents, while Goddard Downs housed more than ten when the entire family was there.

She was nostalgic as Joshua lowered the helicopter to the ground. "I knew we were small, but I hoped we could grow with time. I thought I could help Dad make this station into one of the best in the Kimberley. Now, look at it. Sitting idle for someone to snatch up and do who knows what with." She raised her gaze to Joshua and her voice hitched. "They might change everything, erase my entire childhood, and turn it into a resort or something ridiculous like that. They could do whatever they wanted and I couldn't stop them."

"Stella." Joshua's tone was gentle, a caution to her before she upset herself further. He knew how difficult losing the station was, and the tears she'd cried over it, but this wasn't the time to rehash. He wanted her to remember the good times, not the bad. This wasn't going to plan at all.

"I'm sorry. I didn't mean to dampen the mood. I guess I'm not over losing the station as much as I thought I was."

"I didn't mean to upset you. I thought you'd like to see it. I thought it would be a nice surprise."

"It was a nice surprise, and I do like seeing it," she insisted. "It reminds me of so many good times. But it also reminds me of the fact that those times are over, and that I never achieved my dream."

Joshua's brows knitted. "Your dream?"

"I always wanted to make Indigo a success, much like Goddard Downs. Our herd was never as large, but I always believed we could do just as well in our own right. I hoped we could improve the facilities, make enough to expand the property and buy another thousand acres or so, and then add to our livestock. We could have added tours and cattle drives, much like you're doing now, but I also dreamed of diversifying into renewable energy and starting a small fishery."

"A fishery?" Joshua's eyes widened. This was the first he'd heard any of this.

"Yes." Stella chuckled. "I had such ideas but I never shared them. Dad was working on getting things stable on the station and I didn't want to overwhelm him with ideas that couldn't be acted upon."

Joshua smiled as he toyed with a lock of her hair and gazed deeply into her eyes. "You need to tell me more about your ideas."

Her eyes twinkled. "You'd have to promise not to laugh. Some of them are pretty far out there."

He chuckled. "I'm sure they're great. But why don't we head for home and you can tell me about them after you get out of your wet clothes and have something to eat?" Her mood was picking up and he wanted to keep it that way. *Score zero for the Indigo proposal.*

Smiling, she agreed that heading home was the best idea. She slipped her hand into his as he pulled back on the stick and the helicopter rose off the ground. Minutes later they were in the air and headed in the direction of Goddard Downs.

Thunder rumbled in the distance as the helicopter landed outside the homestead. The sky had darkened and Joshua guessed they had less than half an hour before the storm hit.

He turned the engine off and jumped down before jogging to the other side to lift Stella down. She was more than capable of getting out on her own, but he wanted to hold her. Kiss her. Propose to her. What made him think that proposing to her at Indigo would ever work? It was such a stupid idea.

Her hair was dry but the rain had made it curly. She looked so innocent and drop-dead gorgeous. He lowered his mouth and kissed her gently. "I love you, Stella."

"I love you, too, Josh."

The words were a balm to his soul. *She loved him.*

When a loud clap of thunder boomed overhead, he almost dropped her.

"We'd best hurry or we'll get wet." She planted a kiss on his lips and wriggled to the ground.

He didn't care if they got wet, but he let her go and grabbed her bags.

"I'll grab a shower and then I'll be over," she said when they reached her cabin.

"I'll come and get you."

"No need. I'll be fine."

"But what if it's raining?"

"I've got an umbrella." Her spunky grin made his heart burst with love.

"Okay, but don't be long."

"I won't." She smiled and went inside.

He left her and hurried to the homestead. With Maggie's family still there, the house was bursting at the seams, and he wanted to be sure there was a place for Stella at the table.

Passing the door to the living room, his dad called out, "How did it go, Josh?" A moment later, he appeared in the doorway wearing a lopsided grin. "Well?"

"It didn't." Joshua's shoulders fell. "I need to rethink my plan. Things didn't go as I'd hoped, so I thought it best to put off the proposal for a better time."

His dad squeezed his shoulder. "You'll know the right time, son. No sense in rushing things. There's a perfect time for everything."

"And a season for everything under the sun. Is that what that scripture says?" Joshua remembered some of what his parents taught him as a child, but it was sometimes foggy from years of disregarding it.

"Something like that," his dad answered, smiling. "Dinner's almost ready. Will Stella be joining us?"

"Yes, she's grabbing a shower first. She got drenched in town."

"It'll be good to have her with us again. The family all under one roof."

His father's eagerness to accept Stella was touching, especially since he was still grieving for Julian. *I can't turn back the clock, Dad, but I can be the son you deserve.*

Joshua patted his dad on the arm. "I'll go set a place for her."

NOT BOTHERING to unpack after Joshua left, Stella headed straight for the bathroom, stripped off and jumped into the shower. As the hot water gushed over her body, she warmed up quickly. She didn't linger, although after being chilled in the rain, it was tempting to stay longer.

She quickly towel dried her hair and slipped into a pair of white capris and a light blue shirt. She left her hair down. It was still damp, but there was no time to dry it properly, so she rubbed some product through to stop the frizz. Not that it ever worked in this climate. It was also useless applying make-up as it would slide off as soon as she stepped outside, but she was hopeful that a light coat of mascara and some lip gloss might stay put.

As she walked to the homestead a few moments later, flashes of lightning split the distant sky and were followed by long, low rumbles of thunder. The sky had changed to an ominous grey and she could feel the barometric pressure falling. If she was right, a doosy of a storm was coming. A shudder ran down her spine. *What if they hadn't made it back in time? If they'd stayed longer at Indigo...* She didn't want to think about it. The last place she wanted to be was in a helicopter during a storm. She'd experienced it once before and it wasn't something she wanted to repeat. Ever. She quickened her pace.

Joshua was standing on the wrap around verandah when she reached the homestead. He was wearing the same clothes he'd been wearing when he met her in Kununurra, but he'd done something with his hair. Slicked it back? Maybe. Whatever he'd done, he looked smarter, fresher. He was so handsome, and she'd missed him so much it hurt.

Their gazes met and her pulse skittered. His smile was warm, the kind that simmered at his lips and made her insides go to mush. Was this what love felt like? It had to be.

He rushed down the stairs and gathered her in his arms. She tilted her mouth to his and let his lips graze hers. She'd never tire of his kisses, but the family would be waiting for them. "We need to go in," she whispered.

Grunting, he deepened the kiss.

For a moment she lost herself, savouring every moment, but then she pulled back. "We really need to go inside."

Joshua groaned. "I know." He gazed into her eyes and for another moment she was tempted to stay outside with him, despite the approaching storm and the family inside waiting for them.

He stole another kiss and then grabbed her hand. They walked up the stairs together and paused before entering the dining room. Stella took a deep breath. Although she knew the Goddards, she didn't know Maggie's family, and they were all there. Joshua squeezed her hand before they made their entrance.

Everyone looked up and smiled. Maggie stood and greeted her with a big hug which Stella returned before Maggie introduced her to her family. They seemed a wonderful bunch, although it was difficult not to notice Serena's scarring. Although she wore a colourful bandana over her hair, her skin was disfigured and dark, but her eyes were bright and her demeanour cheerful. She seemed like someone Stella would like to get to know.

Maggie's obvious pride in her children and grandchildren made Stella wish that she could be as fortunate someday. She'd always wanted a big family. But did Joshua? They'd never discussed it, but it was a conversation they needed to have.

She stopped herself. What was she doing? They were a long way from having children. They'd only been dating for four months. They weren't even talking about marriage.

Four months wasn't long, but to her, it felt like forever. As though they'd spent a lifetime together in such a short space of time. All of a sudden, all she wanted was to be with him. To find a quiet place where they could be alone. How she'd missed their solitary rides and long conversations. Although they'd spoken every day on the phone, it wasn't the same.

Frank stood at the head of the table and asked for quiet. Joshua directed her to a chair between him and Olivia. As she was sitting, Olivia faced her and smiled. It was nice to feel welcome, like she belonged. Like this was her family. She stopped quickly. She was getting way too ahead of herself.

Frank cleared his voice. The last few months had aged him, and although he was still a handsome man, his hair had turned completely grey and he looked thinner, gaunt, even. Losing a son in the manner he had would do that to a person. Stella's heart went out to him.

"Before we give thanks, I'd like to welcome Stella back to our fold." He nodded her way and gave a warm smile. Everyone looked at her again while Joshua squeezed her hand. "Let's pray."

Stella bowed her head as Frank's voice filled the room. "Lord God, we give You thanks for the day that's been, for the many blessings You've bestowed on us, for the gift of family and friends, and for this food. Bless it to our bodies, in Jesus' precious name we pray. Amen."

A chorus of *amens* echoed around the table before everybody relaxed and started chatting again. Janella and Sasha had cooked up a feast of Goddard Downs' roast beef and homegrown vegetables with all the trimmings.

Once dinner was over, everyone adjourned to the living room for coffee and dessert. Sasha was a brilliant baker and the dessert cake she'd made from rum and molasses was superb.

The storm was still rumbling around and flashes of lightning could be seen through the windows. Joshua stood with Nathan and Frank while Stella chatted with Olivia. They were within hearing distance of the men, and every time Joshua spoke, the sound of his voice sent a warm current through her.

"You were lucky to get back before it hit," Nathan said.

"Not lucky, mate. It was planned," Joshua replied with a laugh.

"It's going to be bad," Frank said solemnly. "The hands were out checking the fences earlier. Kittredge is down at the river checking the banks. See if we're in for some flooding."

"There'll be some for sure," Nathan commented. "How much is the question."

Stella swung her gaze to Frank and Joshua. Memories of another flood would be in their thoughts, and she silently prayed that this one wouldn't result in any fatalities.

A short while later, Joshua sidled up to her and slipped his arms around her from behind. "Take a walk with me?" he whispered in her ear. His voice was filled with urgency and something she couldn't quite put her finger on.

She turned and faced him. "Now? The rain could start any second."

"I don't mind getting caught in the rain with you, Stella. Come on, let's go."

Something in his tone made her agree. He grabbed her hand and they slipped out quietly.

No one, other than Frank and Maggie, seemed to notice them leaving, but the gleam in their eyes made her curious.

She clung to Joshua as they headed outside. The air smelled earthy and clouds scudded across the sky as though being chased by a monster. The storm would be here soon. "It's eerily beautiful, though it's a little crazy to be out in it," she said.

"I know." Joshua pulled her closer as they picked up their pace.

"Where are we going?" she asked.

"Not far."

He led her to a small, canopied grove she'd not seen before. It was tucked away so that unless you knew it was there, you'd miss it. He stopped at the far end where the grove gave way to the huge sky. Dropping to one knee, he gazed up at her and took her hand. "Stella, there's something I want to ask you."

A clap of thunder directly overhead made both them jump, but his gaze remained steadfast.

Her heart pounded. He was going to propose...

A flash of lightning illuminated him and the ring nestled between his fingers. "I wanted to do this at the perfect time, but then I realised it didn't matter. I love you with all my heart, Stella, and I want to spend the rest of my life with you. Stella Martin, will you marry me?"

CHAPTER 9

*T*hunder boomed overhead, but it was nothing compared to the thudding of Stella's heart. Joshua had proposed. She stared at the diamond ring standing tall between his fingertips, unable to speak, barely able to think, as he waited for her answer. He'd stunned her. Caught her unawares. Although she'd dreamed of this moment, she hadn't expected it to happen so soon.

"Joshua..." Her voice trembled.

"Yes?"

Their gazes met over the glistening stone, and for a moment, neither spoke. Her breath hitched as one question burned in her mind. *Am I ready?* They'd only been together four months. *What would her parents think?* She'd only spoken of Joshua briefly during her visit. Although she'd conveyed her deep feelings for him, it wasn't a conversation that indicated marriage was on the horizon. *What would Frank and Maggie think?* The entire Goddard family had welcomed her into their ranks, but now, Joshua was wanting to make her one of them. *Did they know he was planning this? Would they accept her?*

"I know what you must be thinking." Joshua pushed up from his knee and stepped closer. "You're thinking this is too soon. That you aren't sure we're ready."

Stella managed a small, tentative smile and nodded silently. He knew her thoughts because he must have pondered the same question. Yet, here he was with a ring in his hand. She took a deep breath. "Are you sure about this?"

"With all my heart." His voice was barely a whisper as he pressed his forehead to hers.

She closed her eyes at the tender touch. Her heart took flight whenever he was near, and it soared now. But negative thoughts bombarded her, confusing her.

This is crazy. You can't get married so soon.

You haven't been together long enough.

What will people think?

She inched forward. She wanted this so much.

Most girls dreamed of a romantic proposal. They dissected how it would happen, and who would do the asking. They daydreamed about wedding dresses and receptions. She was like any girl growing up. She wanted to be swept off her feet. However, Joshua's proposal wasn't a sweeping. It was a gentle envelopment, like a tender hand around a baby bird.

She searched her heart. She loved him. There was no question about that. And he loved her, she was sure of it. But were they ready for marriage? *Lord, please guide me. I want to do Your will.*

"Stella?" Joshua said her name gently and reached for her hand, the ring still in his other. "This is usually where you answer." He chuckled. He was trying to be funny, but she could hear the nervousness in his voice. She'd never heard it before, and she found it oddly endearing. He wanted her to say yes. She wanted to also, but was it the right thing? *There is a time for everything under the sun.* Was this their time?

She squeezed his hands and the outline of the ring pressed into her palm as their hands closed around it. Thunder rumbled and lightning split the night sky, but underneath the grove, she felt safe and at peace with Joshua.

"You took me by surprise."

"I know. And if you need more time, that's fine, but I want you to know that I love you and want to spend the rest of my life with you. You make my life worth living, Stella. I can't imagine living without you."

"Oh, Joshua." A small chuckle escaped her. She held his gaze as peace washed over her like a warm blanket, and in that instant, she knew. "I love you too, and I want to spend the rest of my life with you. So yes, I'll marry you." Stepping forward, she threw her arms around his neck and hugged him.

His strong arms wound tight around her. He lifted her off the ground and spun her around as his laughter echoed through the grove and disappeared into the night. Their joy drowned out the storm and every doubt. It felt like a dream. Everyone would think they were crazy. She didn't care. The tug Joshua had on her heart was something special. Something eternal. It was one spirit recognising another. They were meant to be, she was sure of it. "I love you, Joshua."

"And I love you, Stella." As he set her on the ground, their lips met. His kiss was tender at first, but quickly grew urgent. She entwined her fingers in the hair at the nape of his neck and pulled him closer. His kiss was intoxicating and when their lips parted, her head felt light.

They gazed into each other's eyes while he gently slipped the ring onto her finger. It fit perfectly. She couldn't help but admire it as it adorned her hand, a promise for all to see. It wasn't big or flashy, but it was exactly what she would have chosen. She smiled as she lifted her gaze. "It's perfect. Thank you."

"I'm glad you like it."

"This is a dream come true, Joshua. I never thought I could love someone so much." Happy tears stung the backs of her eyes.

"And I never thought that someone as beautiful as you could ever love me." He rested his hand lightly against her cheek. "You're loving, kind, and compassionate. Smart, brave, and determined. I've never seen you falter in your faith."

She laughed. "Wow. You're really loading on the superlatives."

"I don't know what they are, but I know I love with you with every fibre of my being and I'm going to be the best husband you could ever want."

"The *only* husband I want." She grinned.

He chuckled as he lowered his mouth and whispered, "Yeah. The only one."

A loud crash of thunder shook the ground beneath them. "I think we should get back to the house," he whispered while stealing another kiss.

"I think so too, but we'll get soaked. I guess we didn't bring umbrellas?"

"Nope. Looks like we're running through the rain." He took

her hand, and by the time they reached the other end of the grove, the heavens had opened, and heavy rain was pelting down.

They clung to each other and sprinted to the house, laughter filling their lungs as rain permeated every stitch of clothing, but Stella didn't care. So long as Joshua was with her, she'd run a thousand miles in the rain. He was her soul mate and she loved him with her whole heart.

Worry tugged at Frank's mind as he peered out the window. Joshua and Stella hadn't returned, and rain was falling in torrents. Conditions around the station would be perilous. As a flash of lightning lit the sky, he squinted. There was no sign of them. "They should have headed back before the rain started," he growled to no one in particular.

Maggie stepped beside him and rested a comforting hand on his shoulder. "They probably got caught when the rain started and took shelter somewhere. I'm sure they'll be fine."

"They shouldn't have gone out. They knew the storm was coming. It may have stalled a bit, but Joshua knows how unpredictable the weather is at this time of year. Stella should know that too. They should have stayed inside."

Maggie leaned closer and whispered, "But you know he had something special to ask her."

"He could have picked a better time."

"Perhaps. But sometimes these things won't wait. I'm sure they'll be okay."

Frank grunted. "I suppose you're right."

"Don't work yourself up, Dad," Olivia called from the couch where William was standing on her lap, sucking his thumb. "They both know what to do in this kind of weather."

"I know, but I'd feel better *knowing* they were safe." For the first time, he recognised the fear that lay beneath his anxiety. Having lost Esther and Julian, that dreadful emotion was taking advantage of his weakness and wrapping itself around his heart and mind. He didn't like it. It was wrong, but it was real. The truth was, he *feared* for Joshua and Stella. His fear might not be rational, but it was there, nibbling away at his insides. How would he survive if another loved one was snatched from him?

Maggie rubbed his arm. "Come on. I'll make you a coffee."

He inhaled deeply. Coffee would help. "Thanks, love. I'll come with you." He glanced around the room. "Anyone else want a drink?"

All heads shook.

He followed Maggie into the kitchen, and while she turned the percolator on, he braced himself against the counter. He hadn't felt fear like this in years, yet here it was like a spiteful mite biting at the recesses of his mind. *Lord, help me give this to You.* Clenching his fists, he breathed deeply and sat at the table. Fear wasn't of God. It was a parasite that sought to suck the life from you. He couldn't deny its power.

Maggie sat beside him and took his hand. "We should pray."

Yes. That's what was needed. Prayer. Nodding, he bowed his head and centred his thoughts on God. "Heavenly Father, I come before You now, seeking peace. So much has happened and right now, I admit that fear has took a hold of my heart. You didn't give a spirit of fear, but one of power, love, and a sound mind. Lord, although fear is trying to bind me, I don't want to entertain it. With Your strength, I *won't* entertain it. I claim Your peace instead and entrust Joshua and Stella into Your care. I hand my worry and fear to You. In Jesus' precious name. Amen."

"Yes, Lord," Maggie continued in a soft voice. "We do entrust Joshua and Stella to You, and I pray that Your peace, which surpasses all understanding, will guard Frank's heart and mind in Christ Jesus. Lord, we know that fear is not of You, and yet we so often give in to it. Help us to look to You in all things and to live in such a way that brings glory to You. Forgive us when we take our eyes off You, and gently draw us back to a position of trust. In Jesus' precious name. Amen."

Frank opened his eyes and smiled. "Thank you, my love. I needed that."

"I know you did. But God understands, Frank. He really does. He knows how much you love your family and how much you've been through, but He's also with Joshua and Stella right now." A grin spread across her face. "And you never know, they might return with exciting news."

"As usual, my love, you're absolutely correct." He squeezed her hand and held her gaze for several moments. He was so blessed she was in his life. He raised her hand and kissed it gently. "Now, where's that coffee you promised?"

She grinned again. "Coming right up." Pushing to her feet, she kissed him on the cheek before filling two mugs from the percolator. She added a dash of milk to each and handed him one. "Here you are."

He smiled gratefully as he took it. "Thank you. I guess we should go back and join the others."

She nodded, and together they returned to the living room where most of the family was engrossed in a game of Monopoly. They sat on the lounge and watched while sipping their drinks.

Five minutes later, the door burst open and a sopping Joshua and Stella appeared in the doorway.

Frank jumped to his feet, as did Maggie and Janella. "What were you thinking going out in weather like this?" Janella asked, fussing over them. Before either could answer, Olivia sprinted down the hallway and returned moments later with an armful of towels.

Grabbing one from her, Joshua began drying himself. "The rain came in faster than we expected."

As Olivia handed a cream-coloured towel to Stella, Frank's gaze dropped to Stella's hand and the glint of the diamond on her finger. His heart swelled. His son had done it. Joshua had proposed.

Frank lifted his gaze and found his son's. A large grin brightened Joshua's face. He looked younger. Happier. Not since before his mother's death had he looked so content. Frank gave a nod, and reaching for Maggie's hand, he whispered in her ear, "Looks like we have a wedding to plan."

CHAPTER 10

*J*anella couldn't love Frank, Olivia, and the rest of the family more. Their love and support had gotten her through the days following Julian's death. The days when her heart hurt in her chest so badly, and the nights when she couldn't sleep, and tears flowed endlessly. Although she appreciated all they did, it still wasn't enough to heal her pain.

The only person who came close to truly understanding how she felt was Frank. They were comrades in loss, but his loss was behind him, and new love coloured the way he saw the world. Not for Janella. Her sky was still cast in black. Only the children were able to bring any light, and only because she knew they needed her if they were to make it through. They needed each other.

Having the family around for the holidays did little to ease the sorrow she felt. She kept her children close, and they seemed to share her need to be near each another. Caleb, who usually hovered around his grandfather, was always nearby, but Sasha was her shadow. In the garden or kitchen, her daughter was by her side constantly. She'd even started baking, discovering a hidden talent that Janella sought to nourish. Working side-by-side in the kitchen helped to distract them from the fact that things were no longer the same.

Julian wasn't supposed to have died. She'd only ever loved one man. Julian, her childhood sweetheart. They were supposed to grow old and sit on the porch together in their rockers watching their grandchildren and great-grandchildren play.

He'd never get to see those children. He wouldn't even be the one taking Caleb to Darwin to start school. It wasn't supposed to be like this, but she couldn't allow her pain to dampen Christmas for everyone else. So, instead of crying, she cooked.

Seated on the couch while Caleb played Monopoly with the adults, Janella hugged Sasha to her side, unable to help the sense of aloneness engulfing her. Olivia had Nathan. Serena had David. Maggie had Frank, and even Joshua had Stella. When the pair slipped out earlier, memories of when she and Julian were young and in love flooded back and revived her grief. She didn't think it right they should flout their new relationship in front of her. She didn't begrudge them love, if that's what it was, although she doubted it was for Joshua. Infatuation, more like. However, Stella seemed to be a calming influence on him, she had to admit. But seeing them together, enjoying each other's company, made her loss more real.

When they burst through the door looking like drowned

rats, she rushed to help them. It was her nature to help, but she couldn't stop the tirade that flowed from her mouth. All her pain and grief were centred on this couple who had what she no longer had. Each other.

"What were you thinking going out in weather like this?" She glanced at Stella but narrowed her gaze on Joshua. "You knew the storm was coming. Your dad was worried sick about you."

He shrugged, a sheepish grin on his face. "We're fine. Just a bit wet."

"A bit! You're drenched. Take these towels and dry yourselves."

As Stella took a towel from Olivia and began drying her hair, a glint on her hand caught Janella's eye. It couldn't be... she must be seeing things. A trick of the light, perhaps. But when Stella's hand stilled enough for her to get a better look, her eyes widened. It was undeniable. Stella was wearing an engagement ring.

Janella's gaze swung between Stella and Joshua while she searched their faces, too stunned to speak. But Olivia wasn't. "What's this?" she asked, stepping closer and taking hold of Stella's hand. Moments later, she shrieked with elation. "Oh my! Dad, come here. Did you see this? Joshua and Stella are engaged!"

"Calm down, Liv." Joshua laughed.

"How do you expect me to do that? You two are getting married!"

The room buzzed with excitement as everyone, except Janella, clamoured to gaze at the diamond solitaire. She slipped into the background.

Julian was dead only months and Joshua was getting married? He barely knew Stella. How could he possibly think they were suited enough for marriage? Didn't he know marriage wasn't a game? That it was for life? Pain stabbed her chest as she recalled the vows she and Julian had exchanged. The promises they'd made. The love that was meant to last forever. She looked at Joshua. He had no concept of what that entailed. He'd spent his entire life bouncing here and there, never committing to anything, not even the station. Now, he thought he was ready to take on a lifelong commitment before God? He was deluding himself.

The sting of tears burned her eyes. She wanted to speak but the words danced on the tip of her tongue, unwilling to leap from her mouth. When Frank stepped forward, she was sure that as a man of reason, he'd stop the madness and tell Joshua he was making a mistake. Then everyone would come to their senses.

But no. He wore a broad smile and gave them bear hugs. "Congratulations. I wish you both every happiness."

Janella choked on the air. *Frank thought this was a good idea?* How could she speak her mind now? Frank was the voice of reason and head of the family. How could she challenge what he sanctioned? Her head was about to explode.

Retreating further, she slumped onto the couch and tried to assemble her thoughts. They'd notice if she didn't say something. But what could she say? The truth was out of the question. Everyone was smiling, patting Joshua on the back, and circling a grinning Stella as they took it in turns to admire her ring. They were happy. How could she rob them of that?

Although she didn't share their happiness, she couldn't ruin everyone else's joy.

Sasha approached, her face contorted. "Mum?"

Janella reached out and took her hand. "Yes, sweetie?"

"Are you okay?" Concern laced her daughter's voice. How many times had she asked that recently? Too many. It was Janella's place to comfort her daughter, not the other way around.

She squeezed Sasha's hand and smiled. "I'm okay. Just a touch of a headache."

Serena turned in her direction. "You have a headache?"

The others turned to Janella. Looks of concern replaced the joy of the moment. She couldn't be responsible for that. She straightened and forced herself to sound cheerful. "I'm fine, really. It's nothing serious. Barely a niggle."

"Are you sure, Janella?" Joshua stepped closer and sounded genuinely concerned, which surprised her. He wasn't normally that caring.

She wanted to say that she wasn't all right. That she thought he'd lost his mind, but she didn't. She rose to her feet and forced herself to smile as she reached up and hugged him. "Perfectly. Congratulations, Joshua. You and Stella make a picture-perfect couple."

Her words seemed to allay everyone's concerns, including Sasha's, who smiled and then continued ogling Stella's ring.

Janella's heart clenched. Her daughter was so young. To her, romance was an exciting wonder she looked forward to one day, not the labour of love required to make a marriage last. Janella's gaze drifted to Stella. She was as clueless as Sasha if she thought being married to Joshua would be a walk in the park.

Slumping back onto the couch, she pulled one of the cushions onto her lap and hugged it. Everyone was happy again and had forgotten about her. *You're alone now, Janella. You have to remember that. Everyone has someone. You just have yourself.*

The cruel thoughts continued as she sat there, falling further and further into misery. Although she and Julian went through tough times, they understood each other. They'd known each other since they were kids. What did Joshua know about Stella in a few months? Her gaze drifted to where he stood shaking David's hand. *You're making a mistake, Joshua. I pray you realise that before it's too late. Lord, let them see sense.*

She hugged the pillow tighter and fought tears as her gaze caught a glimpse of a picture on the sideboard. It was of her and Julian as newlyweds taken on the morning they left for a camping trip with friends. His smile was so brilliant it took her breath away. It still did.

Julian never made breakfast, but he did that day. It was such a sweet gesture, although it tasted awful and she wound up making something more edible to take with them. She smiled at the memory.

His love made all the difference in her life. It nullified every negative thought she had about herself and the lies others told her. She was indigenous. Coloured. Looked down on by society. He was the opposite. The eldest Goddard son, highly regarded by all. They should never have fallen in love. When he went off to school in Darwin, she'd feared he'd forget all about her when he saw all there was to be had outside the boundaries of Goddard Downs. But he didn't. He was faithful for all the years he was away and all the years after. He never strayed. Keeping no secrets, he even told her when someone caught his eye.

Her husband hadn't been perfect, but he was hers. What they shared often didn't make sense to the world around them, but it was right for them.

An errant tear rolled down her cheek. She quickly brushed it aside before anyone noticed. Her darling Julian. He never gave himself a break or allowed himself to relax. He always wanted to be right. Always wanted to be a 'good son', and to prove he was worthy of the responsibility he craved. He never had to prove anything to her. She saw him, and he saw her, past her skin colour, her family, her lack of education. He understood her on a level no one else did. They truly loved each other when so many said they shouldn't.

She wanted Joshua to know a love like that. Perhaps Stella was the one, but they hadn't had enough time to test their relationship, to see if it was true and could withstand the test of time. They needed to learn about each other, the way she'd learned about Julian. They needed to make such a big decision when the cloud of grief wasn't hovering over them, masking their loss with a promise of happiness. That's what it was. Joshua felt sad about Julian and wanted the pain to go away. If only it was that simple. If it were, she would have easily found some way to make her sorrow vanish, but it wasn't. And jumping into marriage wasn't the answer.

She gazed around at the smiling faces in the room. They all wanted to be happy. To forget the pain of Julian's loss. That was why they were so quick to embrace this foolhardy idea of

Joshua's. In time, they'd come to see it was a mistake. They would see it as she did now.

Olivia approached the couch where Janella was sitting. "Janella, can you help me get some drinks to toast with?"

"Sure." Pushing up from her seat, she followed Olivia to the kitchen, glancing over her shoulder as she left the room. She'd speak with Joshua another time, but for now, she'd let him have his moment of happiness.

CHAPTER 11

*T*alk of the wedding continued at fever pace, and Janella grew more and more concerned. She wanted Joshua and Stella to be happy, but this wasn't the way. No one else seemed to share her feelings, and as the days passed, she was uncertain whether she should speak up or hold her tongue.

Indecision wasn't usually something she suffered with. She knew what was right and what was wrong and had always tried to do the right thing. When things were rocky in the household, she'd remained steady and stable. However, now she was the one who needed a buoy to stay afloat. The pile of laundry had grown exponentially. She had little interest in it. Now, sitting and folding her third load for the day, exhaustion filled her bones. Still, her mind was unsettled. One thought filled it even more than her concerns about Joshua's engagement. *Would she ever feel normal again?* Would she ever feel like herself, and not the pale facsimile who acted like Janella?

Pulling one of Caleb's shirts from the pile, she checked the collar. It was a size sixteen. Her shoulders drooped. Her boy was growing into a man and she wasn't ready. Soon, he'd fit into his father's shirts. Her gaze drifted to the wardrobe where Julian's clothing remained on hangers and folded in drawers. She hadn't the heart to give them away, despite the assurances of others that it would help ease her into the idea that he was gone. She didn't need to be eased into it. Every day she woke up and his absence screamed at her. Tearing her gaze away, she folded the shirt and set it aside before pulling a new one from the pile. As if to torture her, the item that came to hand was one of Julian's shirts.

Looking at the emerald green button-down reminded her of the seafoam accent wall behind their bed. Julian had insisted the room needed some brightening, and being a lover of green, he chose that colour. At first, she didn't like it, but now she loved it. It was part of the fabric of their marriage. She liked her keepsakes, and the walls and surfaces were covered in photos, paintings, and baby handprints set in clay. The way she hadn't complained about the paint, Julian never complained about her sense of décor. Their past was on display around her. There was no escaping it and she didn't wish to. She wanted to cling to those times as long as she could. She wanted to hold on to Julian a while longer, although one day she'd have to let go.

Her stomach twisted in knots as she pulled the shirt to her and inhaled deeply, her eyes closing. Julian's scent permeated the fabric as if it was a part of the weaving. She could see him clearly as she smelled it. She clutched the shirt tighter, willing the scent to permeate her too, to become part of her so that he would never truly be gone. He'd live in her senses, forever.

She heard the sobbing before realising it was her crying. The tears she'd tried so diligently to suppress the past few days finally overtook her. Rolling down her cheeks like a broken dam, she wept for the man she loved. *Why Lord? Why did he have to die?* She'd asked the question a thousand times without an answer. Why did the God she loved take her husband from her and her children?

You said You'd never leave me or forsake me, Lord. Then why did You do this? Why did you take him away when things were starting to turn around? Julian was finally seeing his way in You. He was praying more and believing more. He was trying. Why did you take him, Lord?

Tears rolled faster the more she summoned an answer, and the deeper the silence became until she was oblivious to every other sound, including that of Caleb entering the room.

"Mum, what's the matter?" he asked, rushing to her side. He sat beside her on the bed and wrapped his arms around her. "Don't cry, Mum. Please, don't cry. I don't know what to do when you cry. Tell me what to do."

Janella could hear the sadness in her son's voice as she lowered the shirt from her face and looked at him. He wanted to help her, to make the pain go away. Her baby boy was growing up, maturing before her eyes.

It isn't his place to comfort me, Lord. I'm supposed to take care of him. "I'm okay," she said, sniffing.

"No, you're not. You're crying." His protest came with a stern look. "Don't say you're something when you're not. Don't lie, Mum. I know you miss Dad." His voice lowered. "I miss him, too."

She looked at her son in wonder. When did he grow up? How was she ever going to say goodbye and let Darwin have him?

She heard Julian's voice in her head. *It's what's right, Janella. The boy can't stay tied to your apron strings forever. He has to go out and experience the world as I did. He'll learn to appreciate what he has even more afterwards. You have to let him be a man. He can't stay a boy forever.*

She nodded. "You're right, Caleb. I shouldn't lie. I'm sorry. I do miss your father. I miss him so much. Sometimes, I don't know what I'm going to do."

The honesty felt good, and so did the hug that followed. Caleb wrapped his arms tightly around her and squeezed as if he wanted to force every ounce of pain from her. She hugged him back with equal vigour and they both chuckled.

"I'm not going to leave you," Caleb whispered. "I'm going to stay right here and help Grandpa and you on the station. I can pull my weight."

Releasing him, she met his gaze. The consternation in his expression was enough to prove he was serious. "You can't."

He frowned. "Why not? You need me, and Grandpa needs help."

She shook her head. "That doesn't mean you should stay. We'll manage. We've done it before, and we can do it again. Your grandpa is more than capable of taking charge of the station."

"Or Uncle Joshua," Caleb added.

Janella was silent. Joshua was too busy fussing over his new fiancée. She hadn't heard anything about his plans for the station. If he had any. She tried to stamp down the bitterness she felt. Why was she begrudging him happiness? It wasn't like her. She never revelled in anyone's pain or disregarded any person's joy, but this time, she couldn't muster the substance to be happy for Joshua. She simply couldn't.

"Either way," she continued, "you don't have to stay here."

"I want to," Caleb said firmly.

She looked into her little boy's eyes and spoke tenderly. "Your father wouldn't have wanted you to stay here. He would have wanted you to go to school, and that's what you'll do. I don't want to hear another word about it. I know you want to help, but that isn't the way. Okay?" She tilted her head slightly and smiled.

"Okay," he answered, sulking.

"Your father was so excited about you going to Darwin, to the same school he attended. He told everyone about it." Janella lifted her son's chin with her finger. "He wouldn't want you to miss out on that. You have to go and make him proud."

Caleb's eyes glistened. "I know. I always wanted him to be proud of me."

"He was, Caleb," Janella assured. "You were his son. He was always proud of you, even if he didn't show it. He wasn't an easy man to understand sometimes. He tried to do what was right every chance he got, and sometimes he forgot that others didn't see things the same way he did, but he loved us. He loved his entire family and only wanted what was best."

Caleb nodded. "We were just starting to spend time together. He was going to take me fishing before I went to school."

"I'll take you." She wasn't any good with a rod, but for her son, she'd try.

"That's okay. You don't have to."

"I want to."

Caleb's face twisted in amusement. "Mum, you can't fish. You only ever catch branches."

She laughed. It was true. On their last trip she caught a twisted branch and a rubber tyre. She could understand why he wasn't enthusiastic about her offer. "Very well. I'll ask your grandfather to take you. How does that sound?"

Caleb's eyes brightened. "Do you think he'll have time? I know he's busy with the station and Grandma Maggie."

"I'm sure she'd love to go fishing, too. She may even be better at it than me," Janella chortled.

"I hope so. She couldn't be worse."

"Hey! I resent that." Janella laughed as she hugged her son tightly.

It took a moment to realise what had happened. She hadn't laughed since Julian's death, but here she was, smiling and chuckling with her son.

Count it all joy.

The words wisped through her mind like a cloud. She looked at Caleb. Though there was sorrow, joy still lived deep inside. Somewhere. She just had to find a way to tap into it. They both had to.

"Want to help me fold these?"

Caleb turned up his lip and then smiled as he grabbed a t-shirt. "Sure."

The pair sat folding clothes in peaceful silence. The room didn't scream anymore that Julian was gone. It whispered.

What was loudest was the voice that told Janella to hold onto this time with Caleb, because too soon he'd be gone, and she wouldn't be able to enjoy being part of his life as she did now. He'd be far away, and she wouldn't get to watch him grow, except when he came home for holidays.

She peeked at him as he concentrated on folding a shirt, and a wistful smile grew on her face. *Lord, bless my little boy as he goes out into the world. Keep him safe from harm and heal his pain.*

CHAPTER 12

*I*t was an oddly clear day. The wind was mild, and only a few sparse clouds rolled by. At least for today, there might be a reprieve from the customary seasonal torrents. Stella was happy since it would make her work less messy. She was doing hoof checks on some of the cattle. There was a murmur of foot and mouth going around, and she wanted to keep an eye out for any signs it may have come their way. She was hopeful the rumours were just that and there'd be no outbreak, but it never hurt to be on top of things.

Dressed in khaki shorts and shirt, she perched on the steps of her small porch and stared at the dazzling diamond on her finger. She still couldn't believe it. Joshua had proposed, but trepidation tempered the euphoria she felt whenever she thought of their engagement, which was just about always. The family was still grieving, and her and Joshua's announcement might have been too soon, but they were in love and wanted the world to know it.

The first hint that their engagement wasn't entirely accepted was the moment Janella saw the ring. Stella tried to tell herself it was all in her head, but she couldn't forget the shock on Janella's face and the convenient headache she seemed to have gotten straight after. Joshua tried to assure her that Janella was happy for them and the headache was just a coincidence, but Stella wasn't sure and she really didn't want to know.

It was one thing to believe something to be true and another to have it confirmed. She was basking in the joy of her new engagement and didn't want to have that disturbed with objections. She didn't want to hear them. Better to pretend they didn't exist. For now, at least.

"Good morning, Stella."

At the sound of Maggie's cheerful voice, her gaze swivelled up. "Good morning, Maggie."

The older woman sat on the step beside her, a pleasant smile on her face. "Admiring your ring?"

Stella felt her cheeks warm. "It's vain, isn't it?"

"Not at all." Maggie chuckled. "A woman is allowed to be enchanted by her engagement ring. I was the same when Frank proposed to me. For days I kept looking at it, hardly believing it had happened. Have you told your family yet?"

Stella sighed. "No."

"Is there a problem?" Maggie frowned.

Stella shrugged. "Not really. We'd like to tell them in person since Joshua hasn't officially met my parents yet, at least not as an adult, and it might help with any concerns they have about how quickly it's happened. But I've only just come back, and they live so far away."

"There's always Skype or Zoom."

"I know, but it wouldn't be the same, would it?"

"No, it wouldn't. You're right. I'm sure Frank would give you time off to go."

Stella wasn't so sure. Both she and Joshua had a lot of work to do.

"Are you worried your parents will think it too soon?" There was genuine concern in Maggie's voice and Stella appreciated it, despite the slight bristling she felt at the question. She'd hoped to avoid the topic of timing, but she couldn't ignore it forever. She might as well address it now. She'd probably hear more of the same later, once everyone's euphoria wore off.

"A little, but I know what I feel, and I know this is right. Knowing someone doesn't equate to time spent together. Some people know each other for years and still have secrets. With Joshua, I know there aren't any. We're kindred spirits. It's almost as if I've known him my entire life."

"Didn't you meet before, as youngsters?"

"Yes and no," Stella answered. "Goddard Downs always had great gatherings every year, but I wasn't always able to attend. I was sick as a child. I had epilepsy and my seizures were sometimes dreadful. I lived in Kununurra with my grandmother so I could be closer to the hospital. I didn't live at Indigo until I was thirteen."

Maggie studied her thoughtfully. "I'm sorry, I didn't know. You're better now, though?"

Stella smiled. "No need to be sorry, and yes, I'm perfectly fine now. I haven't had a seizure since I was a teenager. My grandmother said it was a miraculous healing."

Maggie's head tilted. "And was it?"

Stella rarely talked about her past, but there was something about Maggie that made her feel she could share. "Yes, it was." She met Maggie's gaze. "My grandmother believed that God could heal me. She was an amazing woman of faith."

"I wish I could have met her. You must miss her a lot."

"I do. She prayed for me every day, and one day, while she was praying, I felt this soothing warmth, like a hug, flow though me. That was it. A few days passed with no seizures. Then weeks, and months. Still no seizures. The doctors were baffled. My EEGs were normal."

"EEG?"

"Electroencephalogram. It's a scan of the brain to check for unusual activity. Most times it tells you things are fine because you aren't having a seizure at the time, but with me, I would have small seizures, almost imperceptible, going on all the time. Then, I'd get the big ones." Her voice dipped as she recalled those times. It wasn't easy for her or her grandmother. Or her parents who were constantly worried but couldn't be there with her. They were all afraid that every seizure she had would be her last.

"Such a long word. I think doctors invent words so they can look smarter." Maggie chuckled softly.

Stella dragged herself back to the moment and away from the unpleasant memories. "I agree."

"Joshua knows all about your seizures, I take it."

"Yes. We discussed it. We had to. I didn't want any secrets between us, even if I don't suffer from them anymore. I wanted him to know."

Maggie smiled. "That's good. I think it's wonderful you're

both being so mature and forthcoming about your lives. It will make the adjustments to married life easier."

"That's what we want," Stella replied, nodding.

"I'm glad. Frank and I both support you. I wanted to come over and say that personally. We haven't had much time to speak since your engagement was announced."

"I believe you had some part in the engagement coming off." Stella grinned. "Joshua told me you helped him pick out the ring."

Maggie chuckled. "He picked it himself. I simply gave him a few tips when it came to picking the right one. It was mostly moral support more than anything else. It was also a chance to spend some time with him."

There was a hint of something in Maggie's voice. Wistfulness, perhaps. Stella guessed it might have been the first time she'd done something alone with Joshua. She wanted to ask, and usually she would have, but she didn't want to pry.

Maggie's voice brightened. "I should probably let you get going. I'm sure you have work to do. I was on my way to the house to check on the gardens and the chickens. Isobel and I have a little routine we like to follow."

"Ah!" Stella laughed. "Isobel. I like her. She's very precocious."

Maggie chuckled. "You can say that again. She's a little darling who knows her mind quite well."

"Sounds like me when I was a child," Stella replied. "I always had something to say. The doctors and nurses would take time out to chat with me and make me feel better, especially if my grandmother had to be away from the hospital."

"That must have been difficult for you, and for her. It was hard enough when Serena had her accident and suffered the burns you can see on her now. Although she was an adult when that happened, I didn't like leaving her alone. It must have been so hard for your parents and grandmother."

"Yes, I think it was, but they couldn't be with me twenty-four seven. They did their best, though."

"As most parents and grandparents do." Maggie smiled. "As a mother, I always tried my best for my children. We don't always get it right, but it helps a lot knowing God's looking after them when we can't or when we get things wrong."

The gentle assurance made Stella smile. Had her mother felt the same when she was growing up? Would she feel that way when it was her turn to be a mother? *Children*. Stella wanted them, but she'd never allowed herself time to dwell too much on the subject given she hadn't been in a relationship. Now that she was, she'd have to give it some thought. She and Joshua would both need to think about it. *And talk about it.*

Maggie patted her thighs and stood. "Well, I should be getting to the house. I don't want to keep Isobel waiting."

"No," Stella said with a chuckle. "I'm sure she'd be upset if you did."

"Precisely. Have a great day, Stella. I hope we get to talk more."

Stella pushed to her feet. "I hope so too, Maggie."

The hug that followed was awkward at first, neither of them sure if they should do it, but wanting to. Stella felt a need to connect with Joshua's stepmother. Perhaps it was because her mother was so far away. Or maybe she simply wanted a hug. Regardless of the reason, she wrapped her arms around Maggie and squeezed. "Thank you," she whispered.

"You're welcome," Maggie replied.

THE DAY DIDN'T UNFOLD as Stella hoped. Soon after midday, the clear sky dissolved into an angry swathe of menacing clouds that came from nowhere, and not long after, heavy, driving rain drenched the land. With her cattle inspection thwarted, she sought out Joshua when she returned to the house, but he and Nathan had gone to rescue a herd of cattle that had strayed into a gully and could drown if the rain continued. Most likely, they wouldn't make it back in time for dinner.

That meant she'd be on her own with the family for the first time since she and Joshua made their announcement. Although they'd been nothing but kind and supportive on the surface, every day she expected questions about the speed of their engagement, but other than Maggie's question earlier that morning, they hadn't come. One day they would, she was sure of it. If she'd questioned it, others were sure to as well.

With a free afternoon, she headed back to her rooms and did some long overdue cleaning. The washing would have to wait, though. No use doing it with rain falling like it would never end. After dusting and tidying up, she grabbed a book and lay on her bed intending to read, but within moments, her eyes closed. She'd drifted off when the phone rang, pulling her from this rare afternoon treat. Groaning, she sat and grabbed her phone, but her displeasure was quickly replaced when she saw Elizabeth's name flashing on the screen. "Hey, Liz. How are you?"

"Wonderful," her cousin replied cheerfully. "I thought I'd check in with you. I heard there were some pretty bad storms heading your way and I wanted to be sure you were okay."

Stella glanced out the window, although there was no need to. The rain on the tin roof was so loud she wondered how she'd ever drifted off. "We're fine, although Joshua and Nathan are out rescuing some cattle."

"Oh dear. I hope they're safe."

Stella winced. "Me too."

"So, how are things progressing with you and Josh?"

Stella hesitated. She and Joshua had wanted to break the news to both sides of her family in person, but how could she not tell Liz now, especially when she'd asked? Liz wasn't only her cousin, but her best friend, and she was chomping at the bit to share news of her engagement. Surely Joshua wouldn't mind. She bit her lip and let the words slip from her tongue as a grin a mile wide split her face. "Good. He proposed."

"What!" Liz's voice rose to a crescendo on the other end of the line.

"He proposed," Stella repeated. "The night I got back."

"And you said...?"

"Yes. I said *yes*. We're engaged, Liz."

"I'm so happy for you. Didn't I say you two were meant for each other? When God opened the door to Goddard Downs, I knew Joshua Goddard would be making a reappearance in your life. I just knew it."

Stella rolled her eyes and chuckled. "Yes, I remember."

"And you tried telling me it wasn't going to happen," Elizabeth scoffed. "Teaches you to doubt me. I keep telling you I know things, but you never believe me. But anyway, have you told your parents yet?"

"Not yet. Joshua and I want to tell them in person, but I've only just come back, so I'm not sure we'll be able to."

"The word will get out if you delay too long."

"Yes, I know. I'd hate for them to find out some other way." She made a mental note to discuss the matter with Joshua when he returned.

"So, when's the wedding going to be?" Elizabeth asked.

They hadn't decided on a date, but Stella was hoping it would be sooner than later. She couldn't wait to marry Josh. "A few months, maybe. After the rainy season."

"That's not a lot of time. We have a lot of planning to do." Elizabeth spoke quickly. "We need to decide on dresses, caterers, location, invitations, and all that. And I have to plan your hen's night."

Stella laughed at her cousin's enthusiasm.

"What?" Her cousin paused briefly. "Of course, I'll be your maid-of-honour, you don't need to ask." She giggled. "Who else would you ask?"

A grin spread across Stella's face. "No one. Of course, I was planning on asking you."

"Great. So, can we start planning your trousseau? We'll need to go shopping. Do you want to go to Kununurra or Darwin? I think Darwin, since there are more shops."

Stella considered it. "Darwin might work out well. Maggie's family are from there and they'll be heading back after the holidays. Also, Caleb's starting school and Janella's going to settle him in. We could all go together."

Her cousin laughed. "You're already fitting in with your new family."

Warmth trickled through Stella like sweet honey. Liz was right—she had a new family, and despite her concerns about whether they considered it too soon, she felt she belonged. "I suppose I am."

CHAPTER 13

The next day, Frank ambled down the path on his way to the office, dodging puddles of water left over from last night's storm. Fortunately, it hadn't been as severe as expected, and now, the sky was a brilliant blue.

When he passed the mechanic's shed, he waved at Caleb who was hard at work on his bike, a first in months. Since Julian's death, he'd spent most of his time around his mother. It was difficult to watch. Despite Frank's best efforts, he knew that the pain Janella and his grandchildren were feeling wouldn't disappear anytime soon. He remembered well the hollowness he felt after Esther's death. The perpetual wishing and hoping it was all a nightmare and that he'd wake to find her there again. Janella was going through what he called the walking wounded phase. She was doing everything she was supposed to, everything she was good at, but beneath the façade, she was barely surviving.

The vibration in his pocket made him stop. He plucked his

phone from his pocket and looked at the screen. RAVI TAMALA. Pressing the green button, he headed for the shade of the shed. "Hello, Ravi."

"Hello, Frank, my friend. How are you?"

"I'm doing well. And yourself?"

"Excellent. I can't complain. Things are looking very promising for me and my family. The new year should hold many opportunities, which is why I'm calling you. I need to know, Frank, will you be able to meet my demand? I don't mean to pressure you, but a lot is riding on this and if you can't accommodate me, then I'll have to find someone else. You do understand, don't you? It's by no means anything against you, but I must take this opportunity. It's far too lucrative to pass up."

Frank's heart quickened. The topic of increasing the herd to accommodate Ravi's demand had yet to be formally discussed with the family, but it was clear they needed to. "I understand, Ravi. I, too, want to capitalise on this opportunity, but we haven't had time to properly discuss the matter."

"I understand, Frank, and again allow me to express my condolences on the loss of your son, but I cannot wait much longer."

Frank nodded and strode towards the house. "I understand. I promise that by the first of February I'll be able to give you a definitive response, one way or another."

"Good. That's very good. I do hope it will be a positive one. I enjoy working with you and would like to extend that relationship to benefit us both."

Frank took the steps two at a time, waving at Janella as he passed the kitchen where she was busily preparing lunch.

Reaching the office, he stepped inside and closed the door before easing himself into his chair as Ravi continued to iterate the benefits of the proposed deal.

"Yes, I agree, the prospect does sound promising. My family and I will discuss it and I'll have a firm answer by February first. You can count on it."

"Wonderful. I look forward to hearing from you then. Have a Happy New Year, Frank."

"You too, Ravi."

Frank ended the call and placed his phone on the desk. His gaze lingered on it for several long moments, his heart and mind warring. He wanted this opportunity. It was a chance to get back to more of what he was used to—cattle raising—and less tourism. Julian had loved the idea of turning the station into a tourist attraction to increase revenue. Frank had never loved the idea, but he'd acknowledged that it had worked out. In fact, it was still working. Plus, they didn't have space to run more cattle. Although large in size, the station was limited by the aridness of the land, and Ravi's proposal would stretch the station beyond a comfortable capacity if they wanted to produce quality beef. Frank was less than comfortable compromising quality for quantity, but still, the opportunity was a once in a lifetime one. He had to at least propose it to the family. Perhaps they'd be happy to compromise a little. It wasn't ideal, but maybe that's what they'd have to do to snag the deal.

Frank swivelled in his chair and stared out the window, his fingers massaging his chin. He sat for several minutes, considering his options and committing the whole situation to the Lord, when a knock sounded on the door.

"Dad, are you there?"

It was Joshua. "Yes, Josh. Come in." Frank swivelled around and faced him.

His son strode into the room, shirt sleeves folded above his elbows, shirt tucked in front but not in the back. "Are you busy?"

"Somewhat. But never too busy for a chat. Is everything all right?"

Joshua stepped in front of the chair on the other side of the desk and sat down and leaned forward. "Yes. Kind of. But what's your problem? You look troubled."

Frank's brow creased. His son wasn't normally so perceptive. He leaned back in his chair and folded his arms. "It's Ravi Tamala. I just got off the phone with him. He wants to know if we can meet his increased demand for processed beef. He went through the numbers again and it sounds very lucrative."

Joshua's face brightened. "How lucrative?"

"Extremely. We could do away with the tourism aspect of the station entirely and still have plenty of money to spare, only doing what we do best. The problem is, if we increase the herd by the number we'll need to, we risk the final product being malnourished."

Joshua shook his head. "Stella would never allow that."

"I know. Which is why I'm doubtful we can pursue this venture, no matter how much I'd like to."

Joshua's chin lifted. "There is a way."

Frank's gaze narrowed. "What do you mean?"

Joshua took a long breath and sat back. "There's something I want to discuss with you. It's why I'm here."

"Go ahead."

"It has to do with Stella and Indigo. I've been thinking this over for a while now, and I want to buy the station back for her as a wedding present."

Frank's eyes bulged. "You want to buy Indigo?"

"Yes. Stella loves that station. If you hear her talk about her life there, you'd understand. It means so much to her and I want her to be happy. Getting the station back would make her ecstatic."

Frank shook his head and chuckled. "I thought marrying you would be enough to make her happy."

"It is," Joshua said with a grin. "But I'd like to put a cherry on top."

Frank drew a slow breath. "I see. Just how do you propose to buy the station? You don't have that much saved, do you?"

"No, that's why I wanted to talk to you."

Frank understood immediately. Joshua didn't have the cash for the purchase and wanted his help to secure the capital. "Joshua, I can't just buy a station because you want to make Stella happy. It has to make sense for the entire family."

Joshua scooted forward in his seat. "But it does. You just said it. We can't add to the herd here, but we could have a herd at Indigo. The added space from that station would give us all the acreage we need to ensure the animals' wellbeing and fulfill the quota Tamala is looking for. Plus, it would make Stella happy."

Silence filled the room as Frank considered Joshua's proposal. What he said made sense. Excellent sense, at least in theory. They would need to check the figures to see if it translated to dollars and cents. "Are you sure about this?" he finally asked.

"I'm positive, Dad. I've thought it through, and I think it's the best option for everyone."

"What about the animals? Who'd look after them? You can't expect Stella to divide her time between two stations."

"We can work that out," Joshua replied. "Even if we have to hire someone else to help manage the stock, it would still be worth it if Tamala's figures stack up. Am I right?"

Frank mulled the figures over in his head. The cost of a new vet was considerably less than the projected profits of the proposed venture. It would be more than worth it to hire another vet and take the deal. But there'd also be the cost of purchasing Indigo, although from what he'd heard, it was going cheap. Frank liked the idea more and more, but there were still a few questions that needed answering. "What about the two of you?"

"What about us?"

"If you buy the station for Stella, where would the two of you live? Here or at Indigo?"

Joshua dipped his head and studied his hands. Frank sensed what was coming. "I haven't given it much thought as yet. I wanted to talk things over with you first and confirm we can secure the property. I don't want Stella knowing anything about it yet, just in case things don't work out. I don't want her to be disappointed. But if it does…" He raised his head and met Frank's gaze.

Joshua bit his lower lip, a childhood habit that lingered into adulthood. "I think it would work better if we stayed at Indigo. I think Stella would like that best." His Adam's apple bobbed as he held Frank's gaze. "I could manage things there."

Frank nodded in silence. It was what he expected. He'd

hoped Joshua and Stella would stay at Goddard Downs after they married, but perhaps this was an answer to prayer. And perhaps it would be good for them to be on their own for a while, rather than trying to find their way in the shadow of the family. They'd still be close enough and would be working closely with the family. If they were able to secure the property. It could be a win-win. "That might work."

Joshua's brows lifted and his expression brightened. "Thanks, Dad. I'm glad you understand."

"I do, but before we get ahead of ourselves, we need to talk to the bank and find out what kind of trouble Indigo Downs was in, and how much it would take to get it operational again."

Joshua nodded. "When can we check with the bank?"

"As soon as possible. First working day next week if we can get an appointment."

Joshua's eyes sparkled. "I'll call and book us in."

Although his eagerness cranked up Frank's own excitement, it also filled him with a certain amount of sadness. In all the years he'd longed for his son to be more involved in Goddard Downs, he hadn't foreseen that Joshua might take over the management of another station. That had come out of left field.

Perhaps his eagerness stemmed from a need to escape the memories Goddard Downs held. It was a bitter thought, but one Frank had to acknowledge. He looked at his son as they sat silently together. *Was Joshua running away again, or was this truly the way forward? Lord, please guide us.*

CHAPTER 14

*J*anella sat at the table with the rest of the family. They were all there, except for Joshua and Stella, and Janella wondered why. It wasn't long before she found out.

"Ravi Tamala contacted me again today," Frank announced from the head of the table.

All eyes turned to him.

"The deal's still open, but only for a limited time. I promised I'd get back to him by the first of February, so we need to discuss his proposal now."

Olivia raised her hand. "Where are Joshua and Stella? Shouldn't they be here?"

Frank grimaced and shifted in his seat. "What I want to discuss intricately involves them, and that's why they aren't here."

Olivia frowned. "I don't understand. Isn't that even more reason for them to be here?"

"No, and here's why." Frank took a deep breath. "Today, Joshua proposed we buy Indigo Downs."

Murmurs quickly moved around the table. Frank silenced them with a wave of his hand.

Janella was too stunned to speak.

"As I was saying. Joshua wants to buy Indigo Downs as a wedding present for Stella. We all know how much losing the station affected her, and how hard she tried to get it back before finally giving up. Considering that, Joshua thought that buying it for her would kill two birds with one stone, so to speak. He could give her back her home, and we can have the additional acreage needed to add to our herd and fulfill Ravi's increased requirements." His gaze travelled around the table. "I'd like your honest thoughts."

Was there no end to the madness? First, Joshua proposed to a woman he'd only dated for four months, and now he was planning to spend hundreds of thousands of dollars, if not millions, to buy an entire cattle station for her? It was insanity.

Olivia spoke first. "I think it sounds like a plan. I'd have to look at the numbers, of course, and there would be some details we'd need to iron out, but if the numbers come back, I think it could be excellent for us."

"I think so too," Nathan added. "Did he say who'd run the station?"

"He and Stella would," Frank replied.

Silence filled the room.

"Joshua?" Nathan's brows lifted. He looked at Olivia, who seemed just as surprised as they all were. "He offered to run the station?"

"Yes," Frank answered. "He thought it would be best that way. He and Stella would live at Indigo."

"Would that mean Stella would go between stations?" Maggie asked.

Frank turned to her. "No. She'd stay at Indigo. We'd have to hire a new vet for Goddard Downs."

"But wouldn't that be an expense?" Janella's tongue had finally freed itself of its constraints.

"Not really. The profits from the deal would be more than enough to pay for a new vet, and it could even cover the cost of a manager."

His last words dropped like stones.

"I thought you were managing things here," Olivia said, no doubt voicing what everyone was thinking.

Frank glanced at Maggie before turning his gaze to Olivia. "For a while. I don't know how long. It's not that I don't want to keep running this place. I do. However, I'm not getting any younger, and I have to confess that I was actually enjoying having less responsibility after Julian took over. I'll be happy to do it for a time, but at this stage of our lives," he paused and squeezed Maggie's hand, "we want to spend more time together. Perhaps even do some travelling when the time's right."

Janella's words once again locked in her throat. *Joshua was planning to manage Indigo Downs, they'd need to hire another new vet, and Frank was thinking of getting a manager to run Goddard Downs?* The world had turned upside down. She didn't know what to make of it.

"But Grandpa, you said one of us would always run

Goddard Downs. If you don't do it, are you going to hire someone from outside?" Caleb asked.

Janella turned to her son. He had a valid question, one she was sure they were all thinking. Her brave boy had the gumption to ask it. She smiled proudly.

Frank looked directly at Caleb. "I don't want to hire just anyone. I want this place to always be in the hands of a Goddard, but right now there isn't one capable of taking the reins."

"I can do it." Caleb sat taller in his chair.

Janella's eyes widened. "Caleb. You can't take over the station. You're only a boy."

"Janella," Frank said softly, trying to allay her fears, no doubt. He smiled before he turned to Caleb. "I'm glad to hear you say that, Caleb. I was wondering who'd take over once I became too old to run this place. Knowing that you want to take responsibility warms my heart and gives me hope for the future."

Caleb smiled brightly. Janella placed her hand on her son's shoulder and batted back tears. Julian would have been so proud.

"I have a question," Olivia said. "If we get involved in buying Indigo, who would it belong to? Would it be Stella's, since Joshua wants to buy it as a gift, or would it belong to the family?"

"Yes," Janella asked, straightening. "Who would it belong to?"

"The details still need ironing out, but Indigo would become a subsidiary of this station. However, it would be owned by Joshua and Stella together. They'd own and run it."

Olivia looked sharply at Nathan.

"As I said, things would need ironing out, but we do have time," Frank added quickly. "The first thing we have to do is find out how much it would cost to buy Indigo. Joshua and I plan to go to Kununurra first thing next week and find out the details."

"You and Joshua seem to have talked this over at great length." Olivia's brow lifted.

"We had a few minutes earlier today, so we talked it over. I thought it was a good idea, but I wanted to bring it to the family. Joshua didn't want Stella to hear anything about it, which is why he took her out to check on some animals. He doesn't want her hopes raised only to have things fall through, or if we decide not to pursue the purchase. He wanted to give us a fair chance to discuss it without his influence. He also wanted me to say that we shouldn't consider the wedding or his motivations, but I think that's as integral to this decision as the profits."

"Why?" Janella asked, her voice louder than she'd intended. "Why is it so important?"

Everyone faced her and she felt a pang of discomfort. She didn't want to be the only pessimist in the room, but she had to ask.

"Because they're family," Frank answered gently. "And we want the family to be happy. Having Indigo Downs would make Stella happy, and therefore Joshua. If they're happy, then we can be happy for them. What would it be like if we decided to buy the property but not allow Stella to live there? What would that turn family lunches into? Can you imagine how she'd feel? How Joshua would feel?"

Janella pursed her lips. Frank supported this venture, and the family would follow suit. No matter how much the others might want to protest, they'd follow Frank. He was the one they all looked to, the one they all counted on. If he said something, they rarely contradicted him, but today would be different.

The meeting ended with the consensus that Olivia would check the numbers, and they'd meet again to go over them before Frank and Joshua's trip to Kununurra. After the meeting, they'd make a final decision.

Janella waited for the room to empty before she approached Frank. She ruffled Caleb's hair and kissed Sasha on the cheek before they left the room to play one of their new games. Janella wasn't very good at the new-fandangled games. She liked *Monopoly* and *Snakes and Ladders* much better. Unfortunately, those games seemed rather boring to her children.

She strode towards Frank. "Frank, may I speak with you a moment?"

"Of course, Janella. How are you doing?"

She swallowed her anxiety. "I'm fine. Can we talk?"

Frank nodded. "Of course. Walk with me?" He took hold of her elbow and led her towards his office. She followed alongside silently. Did he know what she wanted to discuss? Was that why he was leading her there?

Once inside the office, she took the seat across from him.

"What is it, Janella?" He leaned forward and looked at her with a soft gaze.

She wanted to suppress her feelings and keep them hidden, but it was difficult. Joshua and Stella's marriage, and now the plan of buying Indigo Downs, was a series of misadventures that was bound to end badly. She had to say something to stop it. She had to. Her words tumbled out in a rush. "This is all happening too quickly."

Frank sighed. "Joshua and Stella, you mean?"

She nodded. "They've hardly been together for four months and now they're getting married, and Josh is buying a cattle station for her? It's too much. I think…I think they're making a mistake."

Frank's head tilted. "Why do you think that?"

Her lips parted. Why did she think that? "Didn't you hear what I just said?"

"I did, but those reasons don't make it a mistake. It might seem that things are happening fast, but that doesn't mean they're wrong."

"Frank…"

"Hear me out?"

The gentle tone of Frank's voice made her want to give him a chance to share his views, though she doubted it would change hers. She folded her arms. "Go ahead."

"I know this is a difficult time for you. It's possible Joshua is rushing things, but I can understand why."

"You do?" Janella's voice rose an octave.

"I do. He doesn't want to waste time when he knows his heart, and I believe he does. I think I'd do the same under the circumstances. If losing Julian proved anything to me, it's that we don't know how many days are promised to us. We need to make every moment count. Don't you agree?"

She was speechless. Had Frank lost his mind? But no. His feelings and desires for his family were sincere. He wanted the best for Joshua, she was sure of that. She simply wasn't sure that marrying Stella and moving to Indigo was the right choice. In fact, she believed the contrary was true. "Yes, but I truly think he's making a mistake."

"Do you remember when you and Julian asked for my and Esther's blessing on your engagement?"

She nodded. She knew where this was going. They were so young at the time, and no one thought their relationship would last, especially when Julian was away at school in Darwin, but Frank had supported them. Given them his blessing. She'd doubted he would, since she had a totally different background to the Goddards, but he and Esther surprised them by saying that if she and Julian truly knew their minds, they had their blessing. What right did she have to withhold that from Joshua and Stella?

"I'm sorry, Frank. I'm missing Julian so much. I think my loss is affecting how I think and feel." Her eyes misted over.

"I understand." He handed her a tissue.

"I know you do." She dabbed her eyes.

"I'm sure they'd appreciate your support. Joshua thinks the world of you."

She sniffed. "I'm not so sure about that, but I'll try."

"I'm glad to hear that. And Janella..."

She met his gaze.

"I think they'll be fine."

She still wasn't so sure.

CHAPTER 15

he house buzzed with activity and waves of anxiety swept through Janella, upsetting her stomach. Today, Maggie's family was returning to Darwin, and she and Caleb were going with them. It wasn't time for school to start yet, but Caleb was going early to familiarise himself with the city he was about to call home for the next four years. He'd be boarding at the school, but before he settled in, they were spending a few days with Jeremy and Emma. Maggie's son and his wife had very graciously offered them a place to stay while they explored the city.

Janella wasn't familiar with Darwin and she'd never had any great desire to go. She was content living at Goddard Downs. Big cities didn't interest her. But since Julian was unable to take this trip with Caleb, there was no option but for her to go instead.

She placed a salmon-coloured blouse in the suitcase, and then a pair of black jeans. She didn't know what to take.

Jeremy had promised to take them out to dinner and show them the sights. She felt she was going to a foreign land where she didn't know the protocols, but she didn't want to offend, so she was taking almost her whole wardrobe.

She wandered to the dresser and picked up a small bottle of perfume. It was a Christmas gift from Julian three years ago. Although she didn't wear perfume often since she rarely went anywhere that warranted it, Julian insisted it would smell nice on her. He didn't buy her gifts often, so Janella cherished each one she received, even if they were items she wouldn't have chosen for herself.

The bottle was beautiful, a pale blue glass in a star shape. She squeezed the nozzle, sending a light mist into the air. It smelled sweet, like berries and vanilla. She inhaled it deeply. *I should have worn this more. It would have made Julian happy.* She studied the bottle and was placing it in her suitcase when Caleb appeared in the doorway. He was dressed in a red t-shirt with a motorbike on the front, and dark blue jeans, his favourite pair. The knees were scuffed and the hems were fraying, but he wouldn't part with them. Janella was sure he'd wear them until they no longer fit, or they unwrapped themselves thread-by-thread.

He raised a brow. "Mum, what're you doing?"

"Packing. What does it look like?"

"A mess."

She frowned. "What do you mean?"

"Nothing." He shrugged before sitting on the bed.

"I thought you were taking a ride with your grandfather."

"I was, but I decided to come back and help." He wriggled

closer, looking glum-faced and at a loss. Her heart went out to him.

Despite his offer of help, he didn't make any attempts to do so. "You aren't doing much to help," she said.

"I'm trying to decide where to start. It's like you're packing the entire house for this trip."

The comment made her pause. She looked at the bed, then at the empty hangers in the wardrobe, and chuckled. "I have taken everything out, haven't I?"

"Yes. It's like you're moving, not just going for a few days."

Janella sighed. "I don't know what I was thinking."

Caleb tilted his head. "Are you nervous, Mum?"

She drew a slow breath and nodded. It was no use denying it. "Yes."

"So am I."

She met her son's gaze. Trepidation filled his dark brown eyes. Not surprising. He was venturing into an entirely new life, leaving everything familiar behind, and she wouldn't be there to support him. She couldn't imagine how that felt, especially having just lost his father.

She stood and walked around the bed. Sitting beside Caleb, she wrapped an arm around his shoulders and pulled him close, like she used to do when he was a little boy. "You don't have to worry, Caleb. You'll be fine. I know you will."

"But I don't know anyone. What if I don't like it?"

"You will," she assured him, praying she was right.

"I'm not Dad, you know."

"I know you're not. You're your own person, Caleb."

"But what if I don't do well. What if I fail?"

His anxiety tugged at her heart. He wanted so much to

make Julian proud. It was all he ever wanted to do. "You don't have to be your father, Caleb. You make me proud every single day just by being yourself. You don't have to have the same experiences your dad had while he was school. You'll make your own, and they'll be special."

"I'm scared."

"Oh Caleb...don't be." Lifting his head from her shoulder, she placed her hands on both of his and peered into his eyes. "Do you remember what God told Joshua? *Have I not commanded you? Be strong and courageous. Do not be afraid; do not be discouraged, for the Lord your God will be with you wherever you go.* Although I won't be with you, God will be with you the whole time, and He can look after you far better than I can."

"I know, but I still worry about fitting in."

Janella blinked back tears. "Don't worry about that. I'm sure you'll be fine."

"I'm not so sure. I'll be different. I won't act like the other boys. I won't even look like them." His voice cracked as he spoke.

"None of that matters."

"It does, Mum. I don't want to go. I want to stay here with you. I don't see why..."

Tears filled Janella's eyes, silencing her son mid-sentence. "I have no doubt you're going to do amazingly well at school, Caleb. What others think of you is of no consequence, but I'm sure you'll make some great friends, and you'll have a wonderful time." Being the daughter of a stockman, she hadn't had the opportunity of going to a school like Julian had, and although the prospect of being separated from her son for months at a time filled her with great sadness, it was an opportunity he couldn't pass up, even if he didn't want to go.

"What if I get bullied?"

Janella winced. She and Julian had discussed that possibility. Being partly indigenous and dark-skinned certainly provided an opportunity for any boy who had it in him to bully another, but that wasn't a reason for Caleb not to go to school. "Caleb. The school has an anti-bullying policy. If it happens, it will be dealt with immediately. But you have to remember that the colour of your skin doesn't define who you are. You're a Goddard of Goddard Downs, but more than that, you're a much loved and precious child of the King. You can hold your head high at all times and be proud of who you are. Okay?"

He nodded slowly.

"You'll be fine. I promise." She ran her fingers through his hair, ruffling it. "You can do anything you put your mind to. Just like your father. You're a strong boy, Caleb."

When tears welled in his eyes, she hugged him to her and prayed softly. "Lord, look after my little boy. I entrust him into Your care. Bless him with every good thing and give him peace." Her chest heaved. *Give us both peace...*

It would be so easy to allow him to stay, but she had to be strong for him, although her heart was breaking.

DESPITE JANELLA'S ANXIETY, she and Caleb loved Darwin. It was a change they both needed, but before they knew it, she'd be back at Goddard Downs and he'd be settling into school. They took in all that Darwin had to offer, especially the sunsets at Mindil Beach after wandering through the markets where they tried all types of street food and listened to buskers playing instruments they'd never seen or heard. It was a far cry from the peace and serenity of Goddard Downs with its wide open spaces, but walking along a sandy beach and gazing out across the vast sea filled them both with a sense of God's greatness.

The day soon came when Janella had to leave Caleb at the school. Jeremy and Emma had driven them past the complex on several occasions, so they were at least partly prepared when they'd gone inside and spoken to the woman at the reception desk. She'd been helpful but said the accommodation block was having some renovations done and wouldn't be ready until the specified date, so it couldn't be viewed, but they were welcome to wander the grounds.

Julian had told Janella about the fields where he'd played football and cricket as a student, but she had no real concept of how vast they were, nor how green, until she saw them with her own eyes. She had no doubt that Caleb would excel at sport, and that sport might be his saving grace. Not that he wasn't bright, but she was sure he'd prefer kicking a ball than studying algorithms, whatever they were.

He stayed close to her as they wandered through the grounds of the school that sat high on a hill and offered amazing views across Fanny Bay. She could easily picture Julian here, chatting with his friends, kicking a ball around. Melancholy threatened to overwhelm her again. She grabbed Caleb's elbow and headed for the exit.

"Are you okay, Mum?"

She nodded, a little too quickly. "I will be."

Two days later, they sat in Jeremy and Emma's living room waiting for Jeremy. The day had finally come. Her knees bounced up and down and her hands kneaded over each other. She closed her eyes.

Lord, help me do this. Help me let Caleb go. Despite her bravado, she felt anything but strong. She knew what she had to do and wanted to do it, but her heart and head were at war. Part of her wanted to keep Caleb close and safe. The other wanted him to go out and become the man he was meant to be.

"Jer will only be a few more minutes. He's finally off the phone," Emma apologised for the third time as she set a tray of juice and croissants on the coffee table and joined Janella on the couch.

"It's all right," Janella assured her.

Caleb reached for a croissant, but she was too nervous to eat anything.

"You're not hungry?" Emma asked.

Janella shook her head.

"Anxious?"

She nodded.

Caleb finished his croissant in two bites. Emma's children were playing outside in the small backyard, their sounds of laughter drifting into the house. The size of the backyard had surprised Janella. At Goddard Downs, the children's play area was immense, not confined by fences and brick walls. She had no idea how children could ever be happy in a yard this small, but they seemed to be. She knew Caleb was itching to kick a ball around to help calm his nerves, so she patted him on the leg. "You can go outside and wait, if you want."

"Can I?"

She nodded and gave a smile.

He leapt to his feet and headed out the door.

"He's a great boy," Emma said as he closed the door behind him.

"He is."

Emma poured a glass of juice for herself. "He'll do great here. You don't need to worry."

"Who said I was worried?"

"Your hands. If you knead them anymore, they'll be ready for baking." Emma's eyes twinkled.

Janella quickly stopped her nervous action. "I suppose I am a little anxious."

"It's understandable. He's leaving you for the first time. I admire you for maintaining your cool for so long. I would've been in tears a long time ago."

A grateful smile spread across Janella's face. "Thanks for saying that. I thought I would be by now, but I've been trying to stay calm for Caleb's sake. He doesn't need to see me cry again."

Emma nodded slowly. "I imagine he's seen a lot of that recently."

"Yes, he has."

"I promise we'll check on him regularly. We won't leave him alone, Janella. We'll be there for him if ever he needs us."

Emma's words gave some comfort, but anxiety still lingered in Janella's heart.

Be anxious for nothing.

"He's nervous about fitting in."

Be anxious for nothing.

"He'll do just fine. Everyone feels they won't fit in at first. But I'm sure he'll be okay."

"I hope so. It's harder because he's just lost his father," Janella replied. *And he's worried because he's partly indigenous and most of the other boys won't be.* Once again, she prayed he wouldn't be judged by the colour of his skin.

"I know, and that's hard. But he's a Goddard, Janella. He knows he's loved, and he's stronger than you think."

Janella met Emma's soft gaze. They were as different as two women could be. Emma was a city girl, born and bred. Janella, the daughter of a stockman, born and raised on the land, and yet they shared a bond. They were both daughters of the King.

"I know we don't know each other very well, but I'd love to pray with you. Would you let me?"

Janella nodded. "I'd appreciate that. Thank you."

Emma reached her hands out and waited for Janella to take them. She placed her hands into Emma's and closed her eyes as the other woman began to pray.

"Lord, thank You for Your mercy and grace. I bring my sister in Christ, Janella, before you. Grant her peace, dear Lord. Calm her nerves. Let her entrust Caleb into Your care, knowing that Your love for him is beyond measure. Help her not to fear. Ease her pain and loss, for I know she still mourns her husband. Father, may Your love and joy envelop her and keep her in perfect peace. In Jesus' name, we pray. Amen."

"Amen," Janella echoed as she opened her eyes. A warm smile filled Emma's face as she leaned forward and gave her a hug.

"Thank you. I needed that."

"You're more than welcome. God bless you, Janella."

Footsteps sounded on the tiled floor and Janella straightened.

"Sorry to interrupt," Jeremy said, standing tall in the hallway.

"It's okay. I think I'm ready," Janella said, pushing to her feet.

CHAPTER 16

The smell of melting cheese filled the kitchen as Maggie poured the morning tea, humming the tune of one of her favourite worship songs while Frank got dressed for the day.

"Smells wonderful out there," he called from the bedroom.

Maggie smiled. "Thank you."

Their morning routine was one of her favourite moments of each day. Since Julian's death, there were fewer days when they stayed in late, but the few they had were wonderful. Today was one of those days. It was nine o'clock, though the sky would never give that away. Thick clouds blocked the sun's rays giving the feeling of early morning. She looked out the window and wished she had a different view. A view of the ocean, perhaps.

Months ago, she and Frank discussed taking an extended vacation, returning to Broome where they'd had their honeymoon, and then driving down the coast road to Perth. Julian's passing had derailed their plans, and since then, the subject hadn't been discussed again, but a deep longing to be away with Frank filled her. It wasn't realistic at the moment, but one day soon, maybe it would be.

He entered the room, a grin on his face as he strode towards her. He still stole her breath away. He wore an off-white button-down shirt open at the neck, smart dark trousers, and shiny black shoes. He also smelled of soap and the subtle woodsy cologne she'd given him for Christmas.

He wrapped his arms around her from behind and nuzzled her neck. "How's the best cook in the area doing?"

She laughed, leaning into him. "I don't know. Janella's up at the house."

"Very funny." Tightening his embrace, he kissed her temple. "I meant you, of course."

A smile lifted Maggie's lips. "I'm doing very well. How's the best husband doing?"

"I don't know. Nathan's at the house with Olivia."

She faced him and swatted his arm lightly. "Now who's the kidder?"

"What's life without a little laughter?" Frank released her, and rounding the table, sat down and watched as she lit one of the stove burners and sprayed the frying pan with butter-flavoured oil before setting it over the flame.

"Sausages?"

Frank nodded. "Yes, thanks. What's in the oven?"

"Vegetable quiche. I thought we could use a change. I found a recipe in a magazine I wanted to try." She took the tray of sausages from the fridge and dropped four into the pan. They sizzled immediately. She stepped back as she pushed the sausages around to coat them with the oil. "Are you ready for today?"

"As much as I can be. Olivia gave us the figures we need. If the bank's amenable, we should be able to progress with the purchase. It should only take a few weeks to get the approval, but you know how things can be with banks and mortgages. Sometimes they require a kidney and a left arm before they give the go-ahead, but I'm sure they'll see the merit of the deal as much as we do, and they'll give us the loan. I wish we could buy it outright, though. I dislike being in debt."

"The borrower is slave to the lender," Maggie commented. The Book of Proverbs held many insights about life, finance, and relationships. She tried to use it as a guide for her life, but she wasn't always consistent about it.

"I know," Frank replied. "That's why I had Olivia draft a repayment plan. I don't want them robbing us with interest and a loan term longer than we need."

Maggie nodded. "That's very smart. I'm sure the bank will love that."

"No, they won't, but it should look good when we make the presentation. Five years and not a day more." Frank stood and began to set the table. She loved him for that. She never had to ask. He always offered to help and often acted before she even told him what she wanted.

"Five years?" Maggie exclaimed.

"Yes." He walked around to the drawers to get the cutlery. "Olivia believes our cashflow will allow that."

The timer on the oven chimed. Maggie turned it off and pulled the pan from the oven, placing it on a cooling rack to let the mini quiches rest a moment before serving them. She grabbed two large white plates and dished out the sausages before placing two of the cup-cake sized quiches on each plate. She then fetched the sliced fruit from the fridge. She'd arranged the slices of mango, honeydew, and oranges in a pretty design, and they looked scrumptious.

"Toast?" she asked.

"No, thanks." Frank replied. "Finished with those?" He gestured to the plates on the counter.

"Yes. I'll grab the tea."

He headed to the counter and carried the plates to the table while she collected the teapot, cups, and saucers and placed them in the middle, between them.

After they were both seated, he took her hand and squeezed it before they closed their eyes while he gave thanks for the meal.

They began eating, but after a few minutes, Maggie set her cutlery down and poured the tea. "I've been thinking about something," she said as she placed a cup in front of him.

"And what's that, my love?"

"Do you remember the idea we had about going back to Broome?"

"Of course," he said, wrapping his hands around the cup.

"I know this might be ill-timed, but I couldn't help thinking about it again."

"It was a good plan, wasn't it? I'd love to go back for a few weeks and then road-trip down the coast."

"Yes. It was. *Is*," Maggie said while thoughts of lazing on the sun-filled beach drifted through her mind and filled her with longing.

Frank reached across the table and squeezed her hand. "Then why don't we do it?"

"What? Now? With everything going on?"

"There'll always be things going on. Maybe we can go to Broome for a few days right now. We can go for a longer time later."

"Should I call the travel agent?"

"Let's wait until after the meeting with the bank. Once that's settled, I'll feel better."

She reached out and squeezed his hand. "I hope it goes well."

"So do I. It's going to be touch and go getting an answer in time for Ravi's deadline."

Since everything had slowed down over the holiday period, they'd had to wait another week to get an appointment at the bank, putting their plans behind.

Breakfast continued and Maggie relished the time spent alone with Frank. Having the family visit for the holidays was wonderful, but she'd missed the quiet mornings with her husband. She was sad to see her family go, and knew she'd miss them all, especially the grandchildren. It was a pity they lived so far away.

Once they finished eating, Maggie washed up while Frank answered a phone call. With her spirits raised by the prospect of even a few days in Broome becoming a possibility, she hummed as she walked back to the table to wipe it. She stopped mid-wipe as she caught a bit of the conversation going on in the other room.

"Move here. Are you sure? You and Serena have talked this through?"

Maggie's eyes widened. What? David and Serena were talking of moving here? To Goddard Downs? She scurried to the other room, dishrag in hand.

Frank looked up and waved her over. Their gazes met as he continued talking. "If you're both sure that's what you want, we'd appreciate all the help we can get." Frank nodded as he squeezed her hand. "Yes, it will make Maggie happy. I'm surprised Serena hasn't already told her." He laughed. "I see. Taking the lead on this, are you? I respect your desire to get my okay before getting Maggie's hopes up. Having the three of you living on the station would mean the world to her."

Maggie's mind raced. Serena hadn't mentioned moving to Goddard Downs during their recent visit. This had come out of left field. Where would they live? What would they do? Would Serena be happy living so far from the city? How would she do her talks?

"Yes. I'll tell Maggie right away. I'm sure she and Serena will have plenty to talk about. I think we can leave the moving details to them." Chuckling, Frank looked up and smiled. He wrapped an arm around her hips and pulled her onto his lap. "We'll talk more soon. Bye, David."

Joy bubbled inside her. "Tell me I wasn't dreaming it. David and Serena are thinking of moving here?"

"Yes." Frank nodded. "It seems they've been discussing it for a while and thought this was the perfect time to make the move. Serena's been talking to some schools in Kununurra and they're keen for her to speak to their students."

"She mentioned it to me, but I didn't know it was going ahead." In fact, Serena had downplayed it and Maggie had assumed the schools weren't interested in her life skills presentation. "So, they're really coming?"

"Yes, they are."

"Will the others approve?"

"Of course! Why wouldn't they? We'll need extra help when Joshua and Stella take over Indigo. Plus, they're family."

Maggie's skin tingled with excitement. She could never have prayed for something as wonderful as this. Having Serena close by, and little Oliver, especially, was an absolute dream. She'd get to see him grow up and be on hand to help Serena whenever she needed it. "This is such good news, Frank."

He kissed her cheek and hugged her. "I thought it might make your day."

"It's done that and more." But would it mean they'd need to postpone their trip to Broome again? Probably. How could they go away, even for a few days, when there was so much to do?

CHAPTER 17

*W*ithin days, plans for Serena and David's move were well underway. Janella was back from Darwin, but far from herself. Caleb's departure brought with it a further dampening of her spirits. Maggie wondered if more was bothering her than Julian's passing or Caleb's departure. Not that either of these were minor. Even on their own, either would cause a person to struggle, but Janella was a strong woman of faith. It was out of character for her to be morose and out of sorts for so long.

Standing in the kitchen garden, Maggie could see her outline through the window. Her head was down, as were her shoulders, as she chopped a pumpkin with such force Maggie worried for the safety of her fingers.

Since her return from Darwin, Janella seemed different. She talked less, even to Maggie, plus she spent less time with the family, except for Sasha. When it came to her daughter, Janella was always close. Still, Maggie was concerned. The other woman's retreat into herself was distressing, not only to her but to the rest of the family, Frank especially.

He'd shared with her that Janella wasn't keen on the wedding or the purchase of Indigo. That she considered both a mistake, and that's what was making her unhappy. Frank's words repeated in Maggie's mind as she studied Janella.

Should she say something? Would it help, or only make things worse? Janella was still mourning, and Joshua was moving forward. Their feelings were at odds and Maggie understood that. She was sure Janella didn't want to put a damper on the wedding plans, but she couldn't pretend to be happy, either. If Maggie did speak up, what would she say, and would it help? She exhaled deeply.

Lord, Janella's mourning and struggling with everything. Please help her. Help her, Caleb, and Sasha. We all miss Julian, but they feel his absence the most. I pray that each passing day will bring them closer to Your peace. We don't understand why You allowed him to die when he was in his prime, but help us not to question You, but to trust. Please guide and lead me as I go inside and speak with Janella, as I feel I must. Give me the right words to say that I might be a blessing to her in some small way. In Jesus' precious name. Amen.

The end of her prayer set Maggie's steps in motion. She walked to the door, entered the house, and made her way to the kitchen. "Hi, Janella."

"Maggie," Janella replied, looking up. "Can I help you with something?"

"Yes. Would you sit with me?"

Janella's brows pinched, but she did as Maggie asked, walking over to the table and taking a seat. "What is it? Is something wrong?" Worry etched her dark eyes.

"I think there is," Maggie said, praying once again for guidance.

"It's not Caleb, is it? Did something happen to Caleb?" Her voice rose an octave.

"No, of course not. He's fine, as far as I know. I'm sorry. I didn't mean to worry you." Maggie gulped. She'd already upset her dear friend. Daughter-in-law, actually.

"What is it, then?"

"I'm worried about you." Maggie leaned forward and took her hand. "You aren't yourself, Janella. We can all see it and we're worried."

Janella straightened, her chin lifting. "Don't be. I'm okay. Besides, there's the wedding and the purchase of Indigo for everyone to be thinking about. No one needs to worry about me." There was a hint of bitterness in her tone, but Maggie didn't call her on it.

"That doesn't mean we don't have time to care about you. I know life has been difficult, and Caleb going off to school has probably caused your feelings to intensify. I just wanted to know if there was anything I can do?"

Janella's eyes flickered. She seemed uncomfortable, as if Maggie's questions unsettled her. Maggie sat quietly, waiting for her to reply. Finally, she said, "Janella?"

"I'm sorry." Janella turned her head away. "I'm a little distracted."

"I can understand that. Is there anything I can do to help? Maybe do more here?"

She shook her head defiantly. "I can handle it. I need to keep busy."

"I understand," Maggie said gently. "Being busy does help distract your mind for a time."

She nodded. "Yes. That, and I feel useful when I'm helping."

"You don't have to be useful now, Janella. Anyone would understand if you needed time to yourself here and there."

"I don't want time to myself," she retorted. "Every night when I go to bed, I'm alone, and that's when it's the worst. I *need* to be doing things." Her voice faltered and tears flooded her eyes.

Maggie rubbed her back. "You'll get through this. I know you will."

Janella swiped at her eyes. "I know. It just doesn't feel like it on most days."

The confession was hard to hear, but Maggie understood. Loss wasn't something you got over quickly, like a common cold. It was a series of waves so strong at first you think you're going to drown, and just when you think you'll survive, another one comes from nowhere and dumps on you. Gradually, however, the waves ease, and you survive. Janella would once again float, but right now, she was still being dumped on.

"You're a strong woman, Janella, but you don't have to do this on your own. We're all here to help in whatever way we can, and don't forget the words in Psalm 46. *God is our refuge and strength, a very present help in trouble.*" Maggie met Janella's gaze and smiled.

"I know. It's what I tell the kids all the time. I need to apply it to myself."

"I think we're all guilty of not taking our own advice at times. Would you mind if I prayed for you?"

Tears flooded her eyes again. "That would be lovely. Thank you."

Placing her hand gently on Janella's back, Maggie paused to centre her thoughts before she began. "Heavenly Father, You know the pain Janella's carrying, the sense of aloneness she feels, and the weight of responsibility for her children that's fallen on her now Julian's gone. Lord, I ask that You give her an extra dose of comfort. Let her feel Your loving arms around her and let her know she's not alone. Ever. She can call on You at any time of day or night, and You will hold her up and strengthen her. Lord, bless her, I pray. In Jesus' precious name. Amen."

Maggie gave her a hug. "You'll come out on the other side of this, Janella. I know you will."

"I hope so, Maggie. I truly do."

That evening, Frank was still at the office going over numbers with Olivia and Joshua following a phone call from the bank, while Maggie sat on the verandah engrossed in a book. When her phone rang, she knew it was Serena from the ringtone. She set her book down and answered. "Hello, sweetheart."

"Hi, Mum. How's everything?"

Oliver's gurgling in the background made Maggie smile. "Good. How are you doing?"

"Trying to get everything packed to move isn't easy with Oliver demanding my attention all the time. David's been called in to do some emergency work before we leave town. He couldn't really turn the money down."

"I guess not." Although they were being welcomed with open arms at Goddard Downs, it was still uncertain what role David would play on the station, and therefore his remuneration package was still up in the air. It was a step of faith, one they all felt was of God, but that didn't mean he shouldn't prepare beforehand. "I'm looking forward to having you here," Maggie said.

"We're getting excited about it, too. Not long to go now. In between everything, I've been thinking about my plans."

"Yes…" Maggie smiled. It was so heartwarming to hear her daughter so enthusiastic again after the challenges she'd been through. She was such an inspiration.

"It came to me the other day that perhaps Janella could help me with my speaking engagements. She's indigenous, and the schools I'll be working with have a high indigenous enrolment. I think the kids would relate to her better than they would me. I think we'd make a great team, if she's interested. I was thinking of asking her about it when I get there, but I thought I'd run the idea past you first."

Tears stung Maggie's eyes. How good was God? He knew what Janella needed better than anyone. Helping indigenous kids find their way would be right up her alley. "I think that's a great idea, sweetheart."

"I'm so glad you think so. I think it'll be a good distraction for her. I know the children were her distraction, and keeping up with her work there, but with Caleb gone now, I imagine there's a void that needs filling. And I think she'd be great with the kids."

Hope swelled in Maggie's chest. If this worked, it could be great not only for Janella, but the children Serena was trying to mentor. It could be a wonderful experience for them all. If Janella agreed.

"Maybe Janella could teach me a thing or two as well," Serena added.

"Like what?" Maggie asked.

"How to cook, for a start. I'm still working on that and it isn't going well."

Maggie chuckled. "I see. Well, perhaps when you move here, you can arrange some cooking lessons with her."

"I'm sure David would love that. I think he gets tired of doing all the cooking or ordering takeout."

"I'll mention it to her."

"Great. Thank you. So, should I talk to her before we arrive or when I get there about helping me out?"

Maggie drew a slow breath. "Why don't you wait until you get here. I think a personal invitation would be better. Don't you?" She leaned against the back of her chair and tucked some loose strands of hair behind her ear.

"Okay, I'll talk to her then." The soft gurgling Maggie heard before had turned into a loud cry. "I'll have to call you back. Oliver's fussing. It's time for him to nurse."

Maggie smiled. "Kiss him for me. I can't wait to see you all. I love you, Serena."

"I love you too, Mum."

Maggie ended the call and sighed happily. God had a way of taking care of things in ways she would never expect. *Thank You, Lord. If this is of You, please let Janella be amenable and open to it. Let her see that sometimes You open doors and provide opportuni-*

ties we would never dream of taking, but if we trust You and walk in faith, blessings abound.

She knew that firsthand. Never in a million years had she expected to find such happiness and joy after her first marriage failed, and yet here she was, married to a wonderful man who loved her dearly, living in a place she could only describe as heaven on earth. God was indeed good.

CHAPTER 18

*J*oshua and Nathan were hunched over a map of the area, planning the next cattle drive. After Sean disappeared months earlier, Nathan had reluctantly volunteered to take his place and help Joshua out.

"Do you think Frank will keep the drives going if you take over Indigo?" Nathan questioned as he studied the map. They were considering changing the route, but Joshua was also wondering whether having tourist cattle drives would make sense at Indigo as well. He was more inclined to keep the station strictly about raising cattle, assuming the bank approved the loan, but he wasn't sure what his father would think. He shrugged. "I'm not sure."

"Come on, Josh. You have to have some idea. You and Frank have been huddled close on this plan for weeks, especially after the meeting with the bank. Surely it's come up."

"A lot of things have come up, Nate. It doesn't mean anything's been decided." Joshua traced his finger over the drive route, snaking the way along the mountain range as he considered where to deviate the route for the next drive. He was hoping the change would help improve the experience but also end his boredom.

"Liv still can't believe I'm doing this." Nathan chuckled, lifting his hat and running his hand across his damp hair.

"I'm glad you stepped in. And I'm sorry for dropping the ball so many times. I'm doing things differently now."

"I can see that." Nathan leaned back in his chair and folded his arms over his chest. "Getting hooked up with Stella has been a good thing for you."

"Yep. She's my motivation, all right." As he thought of her, warmth spread through him. They were planning on travelling to Cootamundra that weekend to finally break the news to her parents. He couldn't wait, although a little voice in the back of his mind kept telling him they might not approve.

"I'm happy for you. I just wonder about the timing of your engagement."

Joshua stiffened. *Here we go...* "You mean, with Julian's death?"

Nathan nodded slowly.

"I was wondering when someone would mention that." Joshua grimaced and leaned back. "I knew some people might think it inappropriate, but Julian's death made me realise how fleeting life is, and I didn't want to put things off I was sure about. I wanted to take the bull by the horns, so I proposed."

"There had to be a bull in it." Nathan chuckled.

Joshua relaxed a little and chuckled with him. "Of course."

"Well, who can argue with that?"

They laughed together, and it felt good. How long had it

been since they'd done that? A year? Two? More? Joshua lived in his own world most of the time, his secluded headspace that didn't involve his family. Now, with Sean gone and his priorities changed, he was seeing how much he'd neglected those relationships.

"You hungry?" Joshua folded the map. Even if Nate wasn't, he was famished. They could get a bite and come back to planning later.

"Always," Nathan chortled. They stood together, and leaving the maps on the table, headed to the kitchen. "Think Janella left any of that pie from yesterday?"

"I hope so, "Joshua replied. "I've got a hankering for it something fierce. And perhaps some of those cookies, too."

"You do know that we should eat something proper and that this isn't considered a meal, but a snack?" Nathan said.

"I know, which is why it's good. It won't ruin our appetite for dinner. I heard Janella's making lasagna, and I always like to have two or three helpings of that."

"Me too," Nathan commented as they reached the kitchen.

Olivia was there and greeted them with an amused expression. "You two look chummy," she said.

Joshua stepped around her while Nathan stopped to kiss her cheek.

"Something strange about that?" Joshua asked.

"No." She sipped a glass of water. "Just surprising. I don't remember the last time I saw you both together like this."

The two men exchanged glances. Nathan spoke first. "Josh and I have been coming to a better understanding. Haven't we?"

"Yes, we have," Joshua replied, smiling. He opened the

breadbox and took out the cookies while Nathan stepped around Olivia and grabbed the apple pie from the fridge and set it on the table. "Do you want it warmed?"

"Nah. Cold's fine," Joshua replied.

"Cut me a slice too," Olivia said as she stepped closer to Joshua, ruffling his hair as she used to when they were children. "Don't get my husband fat or I'll have to pummel you."

"Me?" Joshua said, raising his hands in the air in surrender. "How could I do any such thing?"

"By feeding him cookies and pie. You might have the metabolism of an eighteen-year-old, but he doesn't."

"Hey!" Nathan said defensively.

"It's true, love. I know you don't like to admit it, but it's true." She slipped her arms around her husband's waist and kissed his cheek. Nathan wasn't what you'd call overweight, but his girth was certainly larger than Joshua's.

All of a sudden, Joshua had an insight into what it might be like to be married. It hadn't been real until now, but here, joking around with his sister and brother-in-law, he saw into the future. Would his girth broaden? Would he and Stella still be in love in ten years' time? Would they still look at each other like Olivia and Nathan looked at each other? He'd heard they'd experienced some troubles a while back, but you wouldn't know by watching them now.

Are you sure you're ready? A small voice hissed in his ear. *You haven't known her long. You don't even know what kind of toothpaste she uses, and you want to get married? You'll mess it up. You'll ruin it.*

Joshua shook away the thoughts. *I won't have any of that. I'll make it work. It's what I want.* He got the plates and the knife, cut a piece of pie for each of them and set it aside. Olivia warmed hers, while both he and Nathan ate theirs cold.

He stuck his fork into the pie and slid it into his mouth. It was sweet, but not too sweet, and he couldn't help but think it was the same way his life was going. He was happy, but things still lingered on the periphery that could dampen his contentment. He'd feel better once he had Stella's parents' approval, for one. Also when they knew if Indigo would be theirs or not.

CHAPTER 19

*T*hey'd finally arrived. Stella and Joshua had begun their trip to her parents' home in Cootamundra that morning before the first rays of sunlight began lightening the sky. Frank had flown them to Kununurra in the helicopter, and from there they flew to Canberra via Perth and Sydney. They'd hired a car to drive the hundred or so kilometres to the small town of Cootamundra, and now, pulling up outside her parents' home, the sun was low in the sky. A whole day had passed.

She reached out and squeezed Joshua's hand. "Are you ready?"

He gave a nod and lifted her hand before kissing it and meeting her gaze.

With nothing to do but talk with each other for the entire day, they'd shared their anxieties and concerns as the plane soared above the vast land below. *How would her parents react to their announcement? When would the wedding be? Where would the wedding be? Did they want children, and if so, when?*

They'd decided they could do little about her parents' reaction other than let it play out. Stella hoped and prayed they'd love Joshua. She couldn't imagine they wouldn't. How could anyone not love him? He was the most lovable person she knew, and each day she was learning to love him more.

They agreed that the wedding should be soon since there was no reason to wait. They knew their hearts and minds and simply wanted to be husband and wife. There was no need for a long, drawn out engagement, and besides, they both sensed that a wedding would help the family get over their grief. Not that they'd ever get over losing Julian, but life moved on, and a wedding was the perfect antidote to sadness.

Deciding on the venue had been easy since neither wanted a big, flashy do. The wide, open spaces of Goddard Downs would be more than perfect.

The discussion about children was the most difficult. Joshua said he didn't feel qualified to be a father, but Stella dug deeper and he finally admitted the thought scared him. "What do I know about raising a child?"

She'd squeezed his hand and said they'd learn together. When she told him that he'd had more experience with babies and young children than she had, since she was an only child and he had siblings and nieces and nephews, he seemed to relax a bit and warmed to the idea. "But let's not hurry," he'd said. "I want to have you all to myself for a while. Is that selfish?"

She'd laughed and said no. She wasn't ready either. "God

will know when we're ready and He'll bless us in His time, not before.

Their gazes held as his lips lingered on her hand, but a movement caught Stella's attention. She turned and looked at the house. Her mother had opened the door and was bounding down the steps.

"Stella! You're here!" She held her arms wide as Stella opened the car door and climbed out.

"Yes, at last. It seemed like we were never going to get here." She walked into her mother's embrace and hugged her before waving Joshua over and slipped her arm around his waist. "Mum, you remember Josh?"

Her mother looked him up and down. "You've grown a bit since I saw you last, but nice to see you again."

"And nice to see you, Mrs. Martin." He stepped forward and shook her extended hand.

"Let's do away with the formalities. Call me Gloria. Now, come inside and freshen up. You must be tired after your long journey."

"A little," he said, winking at Stella as he picked up their bags and followed her mother inside.

She showed them to their rooms. Stella had the room she'd stayed in over Christmas, while Joshua had the guest room down the hall. "I know this isn't a very modern idea, separate rooms, but in this house, we don't believe in sharing a bedroom before marriage. You understand, don't you?"

"Of course, "Joshua said, placing his bag on the floor beside the single bed. "This is perfect, thank you."

Standing in the hallway, Stella smiled at how polite Joshua was with her mother. Not that she expected anything less. He was a Goddard, and although he'd gone off the rails for a time, he'd been raised to respect women and knew how to behave. She was so proud of him.

Her finger subconsciously played at the spot where, up until an hour earlier, her ring had been. They'd decided she shouldn't wear it around her family until they made the announcement, and despite the short time she'd been wearing it, it felt strange for it to be missing. She couldn't wait to tell her parents, although her nerves tensed immediately at the thought.

"We planned to go out for dinner, if that's okay with you," her mother said, facing Stella.

"Oh. That's fine, but where's Dad?"

"He's meeting us at the restaurant. He got held up at work."

"What time's the booking?"

"Six-thirty, but it's okay if we're a bit late."

"Just as well, since it's after six now," Stella said, glancing at her watch. "Give us a few minutes to freshen up and change. Where are we going?"

"The new Indian restaurant in the middle of town. I hope that's alright."

Stella smiled. "Sounds lovely."

"Great. I'll feed the cat and then we'll go as soon as you're ready." Her mother smiled and proceeded down the hall, patting Stella's arm as she passed.

"See, everything's great," Joshua whispered, grinning.

Stella chuckled, stole a quick kiss, then headed to the bathroom.

~

STELLA SPOTTED her father as she, Joshua, and her mother strolled towards the restaurant. It seemed that all of Cootamundra was in town and the only parking spot they could find was a five-minute walk away. Not that it mattered. It was a nice evening for a stroll now the heat of the day had dissipated. The street lights started to come on, and everybody they passed seemed to be in a happy mood. It was Friday night in downtown Cootamundra, but more than that, it was rodeo weekend.

How had her mother not told her the rodeo was on when they were figuring out when to come? It didn't matter, she guessed. In fact, it might be a good test for Joshua. Would he be able to watch without regretting not participating? He'd told her his rodeo days were behind him, but she had an inkling that given the chance, he'd be out there in a flash. Not that she minded, so long as he didn't get hurt, but there were never any guarantees. Even in her short time on the circuit as an attending vet, how many accidents had she witnessed? Far too many.

Her dad waved as they approached. He was wearing tan trousers and a white, long-sleeved shirt open at the neck. He looked much smarter than he'd ever looked when they lived at Indigo.

Stella waved back, and when they reached each other, she greeted him with a kiss on the cheek. "Hi, Dad. Good to see you."

"And you, love. You look nice." He smiled as he held her shoulders and appraised her outfit.

She was wearing a sleeveless baby-blue jumpsuit that Joshua liked. "Thanks, Dad. You don't look too bad yourself."

They shared a smile and then she stepped back, reaching out for Joshua's hand. "Do you remember Joshua?"

Nodding, her father extended his hand and looked up. Joshua towered over him. Stella often wondered where she'd gotten her height from since both her parents were on the short side. "Good to see you, son. You've certainly grown up since I last saw you. You were knee-high to a grasshopper back then."

"Thank you, Mr. Martin." Joshua shook his hand and smiled. He'd told her he didn't really remember her parents. He would have only been five the last time they'd come to Goddard Downs, and his memories were sketchy at best, although he did have memories of a little girl with long, flowing hair.

"Please call me Jim," her father said. "We should go inside. They've held our booking because I said you were coming. They're very busy tonight."

"It was slow getting out of Canberra. There was some kind of demonstration going on, otherwise we would have been here half an hour earlier," Joshua said as her dad held the door open.

The aroma of heady spices filled the room and made Stella's stomach growl. She'd eaten very little all day and was feeling the repercussions of that now. The restaurant was authentically decorated with deep crimson tablecloths on each of the tables, dark timber chairs, colourful, but dim lights, and wall paintings.

Joshua slipped his hand into hers as a waitress showed them to their table. He waited until she sat before sitting beside her, opposite her dad. The waitress poured water into their glasses and said she'd return soon to take their orders.

After perusing the menus and placing their order, her father wanted to hear everything about the goings-on at Goddard Downs. There was a bit of melancholy in his tone, but he assured them he was quite happy in his new profession. "And far less stressed, I might add. One of the perks of being an employee is that I don't have the weight of responsibility on my shoulders. When the day's done, so am I. No more late nights dissecting financials and worrying about bills."

"It must be a relief," Joshua said.

Stella enjoyed seeing her parents and Joshua getting along so well. It gave her hope that once they broke the news, all would be well.

"Your brother was running things at Goddard Downs before he passed, wasn't he? I was sorry to hear about his death. He had a good business head on him, so I recall."

Tensing, Stella watched Joshua's reaction in her periphery vision. The subject of Julian was still a sensitive one and she wasn't sure how he'd take her father's questioning. She glanced at her mother, their gazes meeting across the table. Unspoken words passed between them and Stella knew her mother was as concerned about the change of subject as she was.

To Stella's relief, Joshua didn't falter, instead, smiling politely. "Yes, he did. He was a great help to our father, and his ideas for changing our business model helped a lot when the ban came into place."

Her father shuddered. "The ban."

"Let's not discuss that subject." Her mother placed her hand lightly on his wrist. "I'm sure there are more pleasant matters to talk about." Smiling at Stella, she angled her head. "Is there a reason for this visit?"

Stella gulped. The time had come. But right then, the waitress arrived with their dishes. Vegetable biryani and curried tofu for her, while her parents and Joshua were sharing three dishes, lamb rogan josh, chicken tikka masala, and a beef madras.

"So," her mother continued as she spooned some curry on top of her rice. "You were home only recently, Stella, and now you're back again. There has to be a reason."

"I agree," her father added, lifting his brow.

Joshua squeezed Stella's hand. She looked at him and grinned, although her heart thumped. "Well...there is something."

"I knew it!" her mother exclaimed, her hand flying to her husband's shoulder. "I told you, Jim!"

Her father's eyes widened as his gaze darted between Stella and her mother. "Stell?"

Joshua squeezed her hand again before she could speak and leaned forward. "Mr. Martin. Jim. You don't know me well, but I assure you that my intentions towards your daughter are sincere. I love Stella very much and I want to spend the rest of my life with her. I asked her to marry me, and today we're here to get your blessing. From both of you, of course."

Stella's gaze was rivetted on her parents as Joshua announced their engagement. Their approval meant a great deal, and having it would be like a kiss from heaven. She was sure her mother would approve, but her father was a tough man to please. If he said yes, then she had no doubt she and

Joshua would have their full support going forward. But would he?

Her father studied Joshua coolly. "Young man, it isn't every day someone asks for my daughter's hand. I'm honestly surprised to hear you say you want my approval. Most young folks these days simply tell their parents they're getting married, no matter what they think, so you've made a good start in my books."

Stella released her breath.

"Now, regarding marrying our Stella. I'm sure you know she's our only child, and giving her to you or any man isn't something we'd take lightly." Her father met her gaze. "We've been through a lot in this family, but we've stayed together. We've supported each other."

Dad. She pleaded with her eyes for him not to go off on some wild tangent and to end her anxiety and just say yes or no.

"I can't wait to watch you walk down the aisle." Her father's words sent a wave of euphoria through her. Her mother started to laugh and cry at the same time. Joshua reached across the table to shake her father's hand. Her father's eyes glistened as he took it and offered his congratulations.

This was it. It was now real. They were officially engaged!

WHEN STELLA'S parents suggested they go to the rodeo on Saturday afternoon, Joshua's pulse beat erratically. Neither he nor Stella had known it was on until they arrived in town, and he'd secretly hoped her parents wouldn't be interested in going. It wasn't that he didn't trust himself. It was simply that going would drag up too many bad memories.

But his hopes were dashed. Her parents were keen to go. After spending Saturday morning eating a leisurely breakfast on the back deck, chatting and laughing, and getting to know each other, Stella's parents took them on a tour of the town and the area before heading to the rodeo. After parking, they joined the line to get inside the showground. People must have come from far and wide because it seemed there were more lined up than lived in the small town. But the rodeo only came to town once a year, and Joshua knew how much of a draw-card it was. He just wasn't used to being on this side of the fence.

Stella squeezed his hand as the commentator's voice blared through the speakers. She knew how anxious he was, but he was determined to simply enjoy being a spectator.

All was well until he saw Sean's name on the program. *Sean was here?* Joshua hadn't seen his cousin since before Julian died, and last he'd heard, he wasn't doing too well, but he must have gotten himself together a little to be on the circuit. You couldn't be drunk or stoned when you were riding a bull. But if you were Sean, maybe you could.

He closed his eyes and tried to push down the dread building inside him. Sean wouldn't be happy that he and Stella were engaged. He'd grown jealous of their friendship before they fled Goddard Downs. But that didn't matter. Joshua was following his heart, and if Sean had a problem with that, so be it. He wasn't riding until mid-afternoon. There was time to find him before then. But did he really want to see his cousin?

But how could he not? Sean had no idea he was in town, but how could Joshua not seek him out?

He leaned closer to Stella and pointed to Sean's name on the program. Her eyes widened. "Sean's here?"

He nodded. "I need to find him."

"I'll come with you."

He was about to tell her it'd be better if she didn't, but she stood and grabbed his hand.

Her parents looked up, quizzical expressions on their faces.

"We won't be long," Stella said. "Can we get you anything?"

"A beer each would be great," her father said.

"Sure. No problem." She smiled and followed Joshua out of the stand. When they reached the ground, she turned to him. "Are you okay, Josh?"

He inhaled slowly and gazed into her eyes. "Not really."

"It'll be okay. Nothing happens that God hasn't ordained. He's growing you through this."

That Stella could bring God into a situation like this amazed him. But maybe she was right. He was still learning God's ways. Maybe it wasn't a coincidence the rodeo was on this weekend and that Sean was here. His heart still beat in his throat, but he had a sense he wasn't alone. He gave a small smile. "I'm sure you're right."

She leaned up and kissed his cheek. "Let's go find him."

He nodded and looked around. Where would Sean be?

Then, he spotted him through the crowd. Sean was leaning on the rail, beer in hand, laughing with someone. He turned his head and their gazes met. He lifted his hand, but visibly stiffened as his gaze shifted to Stella. Joshua started towards him, but Sean dropped his hand and walked in the other direction.

A deep sadness filled Joshua. Was there so much bad blood between them that Sean wouldn't even say hello? Did he resent his friendship with Stella that much? She slipped her arm around his waist and pressed close, understanding how he was feeling. He didn't need to say anything.

"Come on, let's get those beers for Mum and Dad."

He nodded. He could have done with one himself, but he wouldn't go down that path. There were better ways to handle disappointment. He'd learned the hard way and he wasn't going back.

The day passed. Sean went AWOL and Joshua didn't see him again, but his cousin was never far from his thoughts and prayers. He could have gone after him, but he knew in his heart it would be pointless. Sean's heart was hard and bitter, and he was lost. Joshua prayed that one day soon that would change.

STELLA WANTED TO SAY MORE, but she couldn't. Joshua said he was okay and put on a brave show, but she knew him better than that. She could see the hurt and pain in his eyes when Sean walked away.

She rubbed his arm and prayed silently. *Lord, I've asked a lot of You lately, but if You could work in Sean's heart and let him accept our marriage, I'd truly appreciate it. Joshua loves his cousin, and I know how much it grieves him to see him like this. Lord, if it's Your will, bring Sean back to Joshua, and to Goddard Downs. Transform him, Lord, from the inside out. In Jesus' name, I pray. Amen.*

She squeezed Joshua's hand and leaned close as they walked to the bar to grab the drinks for her parents.

THE TRIP WAS SUCCESSFUL, although a lingering hollowness hovered in Joshua's chest, and he knew why. *Sean.* He couldn't get his cousin out of his head. Seeing him at the rodeo and having him walk away, grieved him to the core. But there was nothing he could do other than pray for him.

As the plane began its descent into Kununurra, he stared out the window as his mother's voice echoed somewhere in his memory. *Be anxious for nothing, but by prayer and supplication with thanksgiving make your requests known unto God.* Praying was the only thing he could do for Sean. His cousin wouldn't listen to him, but he might listen to God.

Lord, help Sean let go of his anger and jealousy. Let him see that there's more to life than partying and drinking. He's never had anything good to say about You, but You can change his heart. You can shatter that cold bitterness that envelops him. Help him see that he's not a failure or a waste of space as others have said about him. Show him that he can have a life filled with hope and purpose. Let him be okay with my relationship with Stella. That we can still be close if he only lets go of his jealousy. I guess I'm asking You to bring him to where I am now. Instead of me following him, let him follow me this time. Let him follow me into Your arms of grace. In Jesus' name, I pray. Amen.

Beside him, Stella opened her eyes, stretched, and peered out the window. "We're almost there."

"Yes," he replied. She'd been asleep, leaning against his shoulder, almost the entire flight. He took her left hand and lifted it to his lips, meeting her gaze above the ring that once again adorned her finger. "I love you, Stella. Thank you for believing in me."

"Are you still thinking about Sean?"

He nodded. "If only he could meet someone like you who believed in him."

"Or God."

"Not *or*. And."

"You're right. Only God can heal his bitterness and give him a new heart."

"Just like he did me."

"Amen to that." She leaned on his shoulder again as the plane approached the runway. Before they knew it, they'd be back at Goddard Downs planning their wedding.

CHAPTER 20

*N*ight crept in, and with it, foreboding, as Janella heard the news. Joshua and Stella were planning an early spring wedding. The date had been set, and it seemed that everyone, including Stella's family, was on board with their impending nuptials. Janella couldn't breathe as Serena shared the news she'd heard from Maggie just that afternoon.

Why hadn't Maggie told her? She was aware of her apprehension about their engagement. Why let her hear second or third hand? Was everyone, other than Serena, trying to protect her? But something like this couldn't remain hidden for long. At least Serena had the decency to tell her.

Despite Frank's belief that Joshua and Stella knew their minds, Janella would never forgive herself if she didn't convey her concerns to her brother-in-law, especially if their marriage fell in a heap. She'd talk to him now.

Excusing herself from Serena, she removed her apron and

marched to the barn. Joshua was inside, winding a length of rope around his arm.

"Joshua, can I speak with you a moment?"

He looked up, blinking. "Sure, Janella. What's up?"

A lump formed in her throat. Her pulse thudded loudly against her temples as the words fell from her lips. "I don't think you should get married. It's too soon. You haven't known Stella long enough, and I think you're doing it for the wrong reasons. I think you should reconsider."

It was like an avalanche once the words started flowing, but with every word, a weight lifted off her chest. She'd kept her feelings tucked away inside for so long she hadn't realised how much they pressed upon her.

He remained unperturbed, as if what she said hadn't surprised him. His response confirmed it. "I've been waiting for you to say something."

"You have?"

"Of course. I knew you weren't keen about our engagement. I know you too well, Janella." He set the rope aside and lowered himself onto a bale of hay, patting the space beside him.

She reluctantly joined him.

"I know you mean well, but I know what I'm doing," he said.

"No, you don't," Janella snapped, rising to her feet as her voice pitched. "You have no idea. You don't know what it is to make a lifetime commitment to anything. How can you possibly think you're ready to make that commitment to another person? Marriage takes hard work and compromise, and you don't know the meaning of either. You're always trying to rebel and do your own thing, but you can't when you have a wife and a family. You have to be stable. Dependable. Trustworthy. You have to do what's right for them no matter what. You have to put them first."

She expected him to be angry, to raise his voice in turn, but he didn't. Instead, he looked calmly into her eyes and said, "Like Julian."

Her vision blurred at the mention of her husband. "Yes. For all his faults, your brother knew what it was to take responsibility. He did it every day of his life. He proved himself every day to be a man of integrity, willing to do whatever it took to care for his family." A tear rolled down her cheek. She quickly brushed it away. "When he committed to something, he never wavered."

Joshua stood and rubbed her arm gently. "Like when he committed to you. You were what, sixteen, when he first told you that he loved you? He never once went back on that."

She nodded and was unable to speak as more tears blurred her eyes and rolled down her cheeks. Soon, they were falling freely.

Joshua pulled her into his arms. "I'm not Julian, and I don't want to be. I might not have done things his way, but believe me, I love Stella just as much as Julian loved you, and I'll do everything for her that he did for you and the children."

Tears racked her body as Joshua held her close. "You're doing this because of what happened," she said through her sobs. "You're doing this for the wrong reasons. You don't get married because your brother died. You don't make rash decisions in the midst of grief." Anguish spilled over into her voice, but she was helpless to stop it.

"I'm not," Joshua said softly. "I'm marrying Stella because I love her. From the moment I met her at Alice Springs, I couldn't get her out of my mind. I thought of her every day, and the second I saw her again, it was as if I lost my breath and gained it at the same time. Surely you understand that? I'm sure it's what Julian felt when he returned from Darwin and saw you again."

She was speechless, her tears flowing too much for her to utter a word, but she remembered that homecoming, the look on Julian's face, and the kiss he'd given her. It was a kiss that stole her breath and erased all the time apart. Could Joshua truly feel that way for Stella?

"I know this upsets you, and if there was another way to do it so you wouldn't be upset, I would, but there isn't. We want our families to celebrate our happiness with us. Stella wants it too. She's been so worried about you. She wondered about the timing and what everyone would think, but we have to do what's right for us."

The words were so similar to what she and Julian said to one another when they decided to marry. They knew some would oppose their engagement. They were young, and from different backgrounds. But they were determined and proved everyone wrong.

He lifted her chin with his finger. "I'm not who I used to be, Janella. I have to go forward, and so do you."

She closed her eyes and sucked in a deep breath, her bottom lip quivering. "I don't know how to. Everything stopped when Julian died."

"I know it feels that way, but it didn't. In time you'll be able to put one foot in front of the other and keep going, but right now, you're still mourning, and that's fine. Mourn, but don't spend the rest of your life stuck there. No one wants that for you. Julian wouldn't want that for you. He loved you too much."

"It hurts." Her throat was thick. Pain squeezed her heart.

"I know it does. We all hurt, Janella. I miss Julian, too. I have more regrets about his death than anyone on this station, but I know what my brother would tell me. He'd tell me to keep moving. Not to linger in one place, but to do something to help others, to make a difference. He always aimed to do what was best for everyone, even when it meant overriding their wills. He always had the best intentions, even if he went about it in the wrong way."

Drawing a slow breath, she nodded slowly. "That's true."

"You're a diamond, Janella. Julian knew it. I know it. You were made to shine, and you need to. When you shine, you make everything and everyone around you better."

"I don't know anymore, Joshua. I don't know how to be the old Janella. I don't know how to act as if my husband isn't dead. I know it's wrong and that God loves me, but I feel so alone." Sobs threatened to overtake her again. "I don't know why, but I do. I feel more alone than I ever have in my life. It's unbearable."

"You aren't alone. We're all here for you. *I'm* here for you. I won't abandon you, or this family again. You have my word on that. I'm committed to the life I've chosen. To Stella, to Goddard Downs, and this family. I won't run anymore. This is where I want to be, and you all are the people I want in my life.

I spent so many years trying to escape what I needed most. Not anymore."

His words gave her comfort, though they didn't eliminate her sorrow and pain. "I miss Julian so much, and I'm scared Caleb won't come back. What if he falls in love with Darwin and doesn't want to come home when he's finished school? I saw the place, it was amazing. It was so much better than I ever imagined. How could he not love it?"

"Julian loved it too, but he came back. To *you*. Caleb will come back as well. That boy is more like his father than any of us, and if there's anyone who'll see Goddard Downs into the next generation, it will be Caleb. Mark my words. You and Julian raised a good boy."

"I'm so proud of him." She stepped back and wiped her face with her hand, though her cheeks remained damp even after several passes.

"You should be. He's quite a young man, and we're all proud of who he's becoming. I don't have children yet, but one day I hope to do as good a job as you and Julian did with yours. Having this family around helped, and I know they'll help me and Stella when we get to that point, but for now, we'll be happy simply to have you supporting us in our marriage." Joshua looked at her keenly. "Can you do that, Janella? Can you put your fears aside and be there for me? I need you to do that."

Janella closed her eyes and inhaled slowly. How many people were worried when she and Julian married? But despite their worry, *they were proved wrong. Maybe she was worrying needlessly.* She opened her eyes, her voice barely a whisper. "Okay."

His expression brightened. "Do you mean it?"

"Yes. If you mean what you've told me, then it would be selfish of me to keep opposing you. I do want you to be happy."

"I know that, Janella. As I wish for you."

She released a heavy sigh. "We should get back. The others will be looking for us." She was spent and needed to rest. The day had been long, and this burst of emotion had sapped the last of her energy.

"Not yet. There's one more thing I want to do."

"What's that?"

"Can I give you another hug?"

She let out a small chuckle. "Alright. If you have to."

As he wrapped his strong arms around her, she let herself pretend it was Julian's chest her head rested on, not Joshua's. But only for a moment. Julian was gone. She knew that. But she was surrounded by family who loved her, and for that she was eternally grateful. *Lord, thank You for being with me, and thank You for my family. Bless Joshua and Stella as they prepare to marry. Forgive me for my resentment and negativity. Help me to move forward.*

Somewhere in the depths of her being, a spark of hope ignited. She *would* get through this. She *would* be happy again one day soon.

They strolled back to the house together as darkness engulfed the sky. Janella glanced at the man beside her. He'd changed, she could see that now. He wasn't the rash, undisciplined man he used to be. Julian would have been so proud of his little brother.

"Joshua?"

"Yeah."

"I'm happy for you and Stella. I mean that. And I'll do what-ever you need me to do in order to make your wedding a success."

He faced her and smiled. "I'm so happy to hear that."

CHAPTER 21

*M*onths rolled by, and with its passage, life on the station changed, like the seasons. The rains were over; the days were once again hot but dry, with blue skies overhead and warm breezes rolling off the mountains. However, those were the minor changes. The real changes were wrought with the arrival of Serena, David, and baby Oliver.

Serena and her family had a cottage of their own, just off the staff quarters to give them privacy. Maggie would have loved them nearer the main house or her and Frank's cottage by the lagoon, but Serena and David needed to have some space. Serena insisted on it, and Frank understood that, even better than Maggie. Each day that she woke to find her daughter and grandson on the doorstep, the better the day. She was thrilled they'd chosen to come. David, a hands-on type of guy, was a much-needed help on the station, and Maggie helped with baby Oliver, allowing Serena to pursue her motivational speaking.

She'd not expected Serena to go after this new venture the way she had. Before they'd been on the station a week, Serena had already met with several schools in Kununurra to discuss speaking engagements and workshops, plus the latest addition of weekend retreats at Goddard Downs for children from troubled homes. This weekend would see the first of those, and Serena was anxious. Maggie wasn't sure why. From what she'd garnered from friends in town, her talks had been well received, and she'd been approached from schools in towns further afield, inviting her to present similar talks to their students. Why she was anxious about a bunch of them coming to the station for the weekend, Maggie had no idea.

Serena hovered in the kitchen of the main homestead, every now and then poking her head in to check on Oliver. He was on the floor being entertained by William, and by the sound of his gurgles, he was having a ball. Janella stirred a pot of stew on the stove, while Maggie rolled dough on the counter.

"Are you sure I can't help?" Serena asked.

"It's all in hand, but thanks for offering," Janella replied. "You just need to be ready for those children."

"I am. I've gone over my speech a hundred times."

"The dishes need washing." Maggie lifted a brow as she brought the rolling pin back to the centre and rolled the pastry out in an almost even circle, ready for the base of the apple pies she was making for dessert.

"Okay. I'll do the dishes. I get the hint." Serena headed to the sink and turned on the tap.

Maggie chuckled. "Cooking isn't your specialty, Serena. You know that."

A small chuckle came from Janella, making Maggie smile. Janella didn't laugh often enough anymore, so even the slightest chuckle gave Maggie hope that Janella might soon turn a corner. She hoped the arrival of new faces would lighten her spirits and make her miss Caleb a little less.

"You don't have to remind me, Mum," Serena said as she scrubbed the first pot.

By the time the dishes were done, Oliver had grown restless. Serena picked him up and was bouncing him on her hip in the doorway. "As long as you're both okay here without me, I'll take him for a walk."

"We're fine, sweetheart. Enjoy your walk," Maggie said, smiling.

After Serena and Oliver left, Maggie turned to Janella and chuckled. "I'm not sure where I failed, but I sure hope you have more success than me with teaching her to cook."

Janella chuckled, too. "It's a challenge, that's for sure."

Working with Janella felt almost like old times, except for the conversation, which was more subdued and less frequent than it used to be. Janella seemed to have so much on her mind, so much to handle, and yet she wasn't talking or allowing anyone to get close enough to share her burden. It grieved Maggie to witness it. She knew full well that in times of struggle, a helping hand could make all the difference. Janella knew it too. Still, there was a difference between knowing something and doing it, and right now, Janella was still in a state of inaction.

"Thank you," Maggie said softly as she placed the top piece of dough on the pie.

"For what?" Janella asked, her forehead creasing.

"For agreeing to all of this. Cooking for ten extra mouths. You agreed without question." Maggie turned and met Janella's gaze. "It means a lot to me that you're willing to help Serena, despite the pressure it places on you."

Janella shrugged. "It's just a few extra heads and a slightly different menu. I actually feel a special kinship with this project, so it's not a burden." She placed the spatula she was using to spread the cheesecake batter on a plate.

"I'm glad to hear that," Maggie said.

"Most people don't see value in helping indigenous kids, so any interest shown is good. So many of our kids are left to fend for themselves and they end up the same as their parents. In trouble. Serena sees children who need to be shown that they can rise above their situation. I think it's great. It's not easy being indigenous in a mainly white society."

Maggie was silent. She couldn't imagine what life was like for Janella or the other indigenous folk on the station. She herself didn't see them as different, but hearing Janella speak, she realised that there was still a definite demarcation between one person and another based on their ethnicity.

"God made mankind in His image," she said.

"Out of the dust He made them," Janella replied. "It's just a pity that some people forget that dust has many different shades." She chuckled softly. "I'm glad you taught your children differently, Maggie. That people like Serena are willing to help kids that others would simply cast aside. I'll help this venture in any way I can. Just name it."

Maggie's heart warmed. Perhaps this was the way God intended for Janella to awaken from her sorrow. It was the most spirit she'd seen in ages from her friend, and she would do whatever it took to keep it going. Perhaps there was more that Janella could do with the project? She'd make a mental note to speak with Serena.

A SHORT WHILE LATER, Janella stood with Serena under the large shade tree outside the homestead waiting for the children to arrive. They'd received word from one of the hands that they were almost here. Moments later, an old, white minibus pulled up outside the main homestead, sending a cloud of dust billowing into the air. The sides of the bus had turned red from the dust, but it seemed to have managed the rutted road without problem.

The children were subdued as, one by one, they climbed out of the bus and gazed around. There were ten of them, ranging in age from six to fifteen. They were dressed in shorts and t-shirts, and most had bare feet.

Although indigenous, these kids had been born and raised in Kununurra. They weren't familiar with the land, although it was in their blood. Their ancestors lived off the land and knew more about the seasons and animals than most cattle station owners, yet the old ways were dying. The kids of this generation filled their days with television and iPads, given to them by the government who thought they were doing something good, but it was slowly killing the kids' spirit.

"Good morning, children." Serena greeted the group with a smile, but her hands clung to each other tightly in front of her.

Janella gave her an encouraging nod.

"Good morning," the children muttered back. Most avoided direct eye contact and stared at the ground.

"Welcome to Goddard Downs," Serena continued. "We're excited to have you here and we hope you have a great weekend. My name's Serena. You've probably heard me speak at your school." She turned to Janella. "This is Janella, and Goddard Downs has been her home since she was a girl. She's going to be spending a lot of time with you over the weekend."

Janella lifted her hand and gave a wave.

"For the next two days, you're going to find out what life's like on a cattle station. We've got some special activities lined up, like cooking, feeding the animals, learning to ride a horse, and perhaps even going on a cattle drive. All of this is thanks to our host, Mr. Goddard."

Having just joined them, Frank stepped forward and smiled. "Welcome, children! We're happy to have you here with us and hope you have a great time. This station's been in my family for three generations, and we're very proud of it. It's beautiful country, and I hope you enjoy all that it has to offer."

When he stepped aside, the adults greeted each of the children in turn and learned their names, but as Janella looked at their faces, some smiling, some reserved, others calculating, her thoughts turned to Caleb.

He was about the same age as a few of them. It had been months since she'd seen him in person. Skype was great, but it didn't compare with talking face to face. He assured her he was fine, although he missed her. He'd made some friends and was enjoying the various sports. Not so much Maths and English, but that didn't surprise her. He'd never been overly studious. He'd rather be out with his grandfather, tinkering with things.

She hoped these kids would enjoy their time here. As far as she was concerned, there was no better place to grow up. She and her kids had been spoiled.

A few minutes later, Stella and Joshua arrived, and after being introduced to the children, they took them on a short walking tour of the property. They'd have a longer tour later, but Janella guessed most would be happy seeing the farm animals. A new litter of piglets had arrived the day before, and they were so cute.

Serena followed behind with the teacher who'd accompanied the children, and Frank excused himself and said he'd be back a little later. There was something he needed to attend to with Maggie. Everyone had their place. Janella's was in the kitchen. She needed to get moving on lunch if it was going to be ready on time.

She enjoyed the quiet of the kitchen during the day. Although there was always a lot to do, the silence made the act of preparing a meal almost therapeutic. She could clear her mind and concentrate on only what was in front of her. She didn't have to think of Caleb. She didn't have to think about Julian. All she had to think about was cutting vegetables and stirring meat. Sometimes it was good to have an empty mind. She would think about everything else when the meal was over.

She kneaded the minced meat for the hamburger patties in

a large bowl. There was something soothing about the way the mixture oozed through her fingers. She progressively added a variety of herbs and spices and was daydreaming when the kitchen door squeaked open.

She glanced up. A youth hovered in the doorway. She stopped kneading and looked at him. Shaggy brown hair fell over his face, half obscuring his dark eyes. "Hello," she said.

He gave the tiniest of nods. "What're you doing?"

"I could ask you the same thing," Janella replied.

"You work here."

It wasn't a question, more like a statement. Janella leaned against the counter and folded her arms. "I live here. This is my kitchen."

The boy grunted. He was fourteen, perhaps fifteen. Taller than her, but lankier. Much lankier. The clothes he wore looked like hand-me-downs and hung on his shoulders.

"What's your name?" She tried to remember. It was on the tip of her tongue. *John? Josh?*

"Why's it important?"

"I like to know who I'm talking to, that's all," Janella replied lightly.

He didn't answer, just stood there, gazing around, taking everything in.

"What brought you here?"

He shrugged.

A smile tipped her lips as she returned her focus to the hamburger mince. "You're not much of a talker, are you? That's okay. You don't have to talk, but tell me, why aren't you with the others?"

"Cows bore me," the boy finally replied, stepping fully into the kitchen and propping against the wall.

"They bore me too, which is why I'm in here." She let out a small chuckle.

"What're you making?"

"Hamburgers." She gave the mince one final knead, then grabbed a handful and formed it into a patty.

"My mum used to make burgers," the boy said glumly, then immediately went silent.

Janella looked over at him. "Did she? Did you help her?"

"Sometimes."

"Would you like to help me?"

A spark ignited in his eyes. Janella smiled as he walked over and stood at her side. "What do you need me to do?"

"Chop some lettuce?"

"I can do that."

"First," Janella said, grabbing another handful of mince, "you need to wash your hands, and then I have to know what to call you. No assistant of mine gets to walk around my kitchen nameless."

The boy smiled, a small smile, but a smile, nonetheless. "Jonah."

"Nice to meet you, Jonah. Now, let's get you to work. But tell me, does anyone know you're here? I don't want anyone worrying about you."

"I asked that lady if I could go for a walk. You know. The one with the funny face."

Janella cringed. She hated anyone commenting negatively on Serena's face, although it was bound to happen. Hopefully in time, he and the other children would see past the scars and see the wonderful person Serena was and be motivated by her resilience. She nodded. "That's good. We don't have to worry."

With Jonah working beside her, Janella couldn't help but think of Caleb, although he was nothing like her son. She learned that his mother had died five years earlier, when he was ten. He was an only child and pretty much looked after himself since his father was drunk all the time.

"You're a young man, Jonah. What do you plan to do with your life when you finish school?"

"Nothing."

His dismal response tugged at her heart. "You can be anything you want to be."

He looked up, his gaze glassy. "My mum used to say that."

"Your mother was right. You can be anything you want."

He shook his head. "No, I can't. I'm not good at anything."

"What're you talking about? You've just helped me prepare lunch for everyone and you did a great job!"

"I don't get good grades."

"Grades aren't everything," Janella insisted. "They can help, but it's not the end of the world if you don't know how to do algebra."

Jonah laughed.

"Ah! A laugh. You have a handsome smile, Jonah. You should show it more often."

His gaze dropped to the hamburger bun in his hand. "You sound just like her."

"Is that why you came in here?"

He grew still and a tear fell on his hand. He quickly brushed it away. "No."

A deep sense of sorrow grew inside her. The boy before her

was still mourning. He missed his mother, that was clear, even if he didn't want to admit it. If Janella could help him, she would. "Keep cutting," she said exuberantly. "We have a lot of hungry mouths headed our way. We need to have everything on the table in ten minutes. Can I count on you to get this done?"

Jonah lifted his head and smiled. "Yes, ma'am!"

CHAPTER 22

$\mathcal{K}$ookaburras laughing heralded the dawn of a new day. The sun peeked over the horizon, its rays filtering through the trees and into the homestead, casting it in a warm light. The station was waking up, most of the staff were already about their business, and by the sound of dishes clattering in the kitchen when Joshua passed, Janella was already preparing breakfast for everyone, including the extra kids.

But he didn't want to see anyone. He needed some time to think. Alone. Yesterday had been an eye opener. The kids from town had made him rethink whether he was truly ready to settle down and have a family. What if he messed up and his and Stella's kids ended up like them? Perhaps Janella had been right. Did he really know what he was doing?

He headed to the stables and was saddling his horse when Stella walked towards him. She was wearing khaki shorts and shirt, and brown, lace-up ankle boots. Her high ponytail swished against her shoulders in time with her step, and she looked so hot that for a second, he simply couldn't breathe.

Her face lit up in a smile. "Hey, handsome. Where're you off to?"

He gulped. It would be easy not to go. He closed his eyes and gulped again. No. He needed thinking time. "For a ride."

She traced her finger down his arm. "I'd come with you if I didn't have to check on the calves." Her forehead creased. "Are you okay, Josh? You look a bit downcast."

He blew out a breath. "Yeah. I'm fine."

"Are you sure? Prove it." She tilted her face upwards, and as she closed her eyes, her lips puckered.

Oh, she shouldn't have done that. She rendered him as helpless as a small babe. His chest heaved, and casting his doubts aside, he threw his arms around her and kissed her hard. "There. Does that prove it?" he whispered against her lips.

She chuckled. "I think so. A bit longer, just to be sure."

"You're wicked, Stella Martin." His mouth pressed harder, capturing hers, sweeping his doubts aside. "Are you sure now?"

"Yes. I think you're fine." She grinned playfully and pulled away. "I need to check those calves. Come with me?"

"Sure. I can take a ride later." He removed the saddle and led Flame into the paddock. "Don't go far, boy." He gave the horse a rub and sent him off with a gentle tap.

Taking Stella's hand, they strolled along the track to the holding paddock where the new calves spent their first few weeks with their mothers. They were precious livestock, and Stella wanted them close so she could monitor them for any sign of disease or illness, which was impossible to do if they were out with the main herd.

But as they walked, his thoughts from earlier returned. He had to talk with her. He thumbed the ring on her finger and cleared his throat. "Stella, there's something I need to talk to you about."

She looked up. Panic filled her face. "What is it, Josh? Don't you want to get married? Is that it?"

He stopped walking and faced her. "No. That's not it at all. I'd marry you this instant if I could. I want nothing more than to marry you, Stella."

She sighed with relief. "Then what?"

His throat felt thick and his lips dry. He rubbed his hand along his jaw. He had to say it. He couldn't stop now. "I'm not ready to have kids."

She blinked rapidly and then laughed. "Oh, Josh."

"Don't laugh, Stella. This is serious. Seeing these kids, I don't know if I'm equipped to deal with children yet. I could so easily stuff up. And I don't want to."

She rubbed his arms and looked deep into his eyes. "We've talked about this before. I see a great man in you, Joshua Goddard. I see a wonderful husband and a wonderful father. But if you don't feel ready for children, then we don't have to have them right away. We can be careful, take precautions, until we feel ready. There's no hurry. It can just be you and me for however long we want."

He blew out a slow breath. "Oh Stella. You always make me feel better. I don't know why I get so anxious."

She smiled. *"Be anxious for nothing, but in everything by prayer and supplication, with thanksgiving, let your requests be made known to God; and the peace of God, which surpasses all understanding, will guard your hearts and minds through Christ Jesus."*

He chuckled. "You're right. I need to trust Him more. You're good for me, Stella. Don't ever stop reminding me to look up. I want to be a godly husband for you, but I'm afraid I'm lacking."

"No, you're not. God knows your heart, and I'm sure He sees one that is seeking after Him. And that's all that matters."

He slipped his arms gently around her waist. "Thank you," he whispered before gently pressing his lips to hers. If she believed in him, if she could see it, then he could believe it. Tightening his hold, he kissed her again, until a small voice shouted, "Uncle Josh!"

He released Stella and chuckled as Issie bounded towards them, hands covering her mouth as she giggled. "You were kissing Auntie Stella!"

He winked at Stella as he ruffled Isobel's hair. "Yes, I was."

She raised her eyes in a bashful glance but continued giggling.

"What're you doing out here at this time of the morning, little Issie?" he asked.

"I was going for a walk with Mummy and Daddy. They always go for a walk in the morning and I never get to come, but today I made them promise to take me."

Joshua gazed around. "Where are they?"

"Coming. They're slow pokes."

"Oh."

Just then, Nathan and Olivia, as well as William, who was perched on Olivia's hip, appeared in the distance, and began hurrying towards them. The sun was at their back and Joshua had to hold his hand against his forehead.

"She got away from us," Nathan panted when he finally reached them. He crouched down in front of Isobel. "Now what did I tell you?"

Her head dropped. "I have to stay close if I want to go on the walk with you and Mummy."

"So why didn't you?"

"I wanted to play hide-n-seek."

A moment later, Olivia reached them. "Hide-n-seek, eh? You almost gave me a heart attack, disappearing like that." She looked at Joshua and Stella. "Sorry if Isobel interrupted anything."

"It's quite all right," Stella replied, grinning. "She proved my point."

Her point? It took a minute for Joshua to understand what she meant. The ease with which he'd handled Isobel. The simplicity of it, and how naturally he'd ruffled her hair and talked with her. It felt natural. Maybe there was more of a father in him than he thought.

"We'll leave you alone," Nathan said, taking Isobel's hand.

"Catch you later." Joshua tipped his hat and nodded. They were doing a riding session with the children later that morning. He'd been dreading it, but now, he was actually looking forward to it. Maybe he could help those kids after all. Maybe he could warm to them like he warmed to Isobel. Maybe being a father wouldn't be as scary as he thought.

The sun was fully up and the sky was a brilliant blue. He took Stella's hand and kissed it. "It's going to be a beautiful day."

She chuckled. "Sure is."

LATER, after she and Joshua had returned from checking the calves and he had left to prepare for the riding lessons, Stella was checking her supplies in the shed, but her thoughts were on Joshua. His honesty was heartwarming, and even though he'd given her a heart attack when she thought he was going to break their engagement, with every step they took towards each other, the more excited and the more in love she felt, as if God was stitching them together in His great tapestry. There would be rough patches, of course. What relationship didn't have those? But with God, they could make it through anything.

She headed to the house, but at the last moment decided to detour via the piglets and came face to face with Olivia. "Oh, I didn't expect to see you here."

"Isobel and William wanted to look at the new piggies."

Stella smiled at the children. "They're very cute, aren't they?"

"Yes," Isobel replied. "I like the way they oink and run around. Can I hold one?"

Stella looked to Olivia, who shrugged. "Okay, but you'll get your pretty dress dirty."

"That doesn't matter. Mummy will wash it."

Olivia chuckled and shook her head.

"Okay, come with me. William, do you want to hold one, too?" Stella asked.

He nodded and took her hand.

Olivia followed and helped settle a small piglet into William's arms, while Stella placed one into Isobel's. The look of joy on the children's faces made her heart glad, and a longing for her own children grew within her. But she needed to be patient. She'd promised Joshua there would be no hurry. She had to honour that.

As the four headed to the homestead for morning tea a short while later, Isobel and William ran ahead, leaving Olivia and Stella to stroll along behind them. "Thank you, Stella," Olivia said, smiling.

"What for?"

"For bearing with my brother. I thought he'd be wild for the rest of his life. It wasn't what I wanted, and I prayed he'd settle and find his way. I never thought it would happen so quickly. I'm glad you had what it took to make him see his way forward and stop languishing in the past. God used you, and I'm sure He'll keep using you to bring out the best in Josh."

"Wow. Thank you." She honestly didn't know what to say.

"I mean it. I have no doubts that you, Miss Martin, are a Goddard woman waiting to happen. It takes a certain strength to lead the lives we lead and love the men we do, but I see it in you. It's a God-given gift, to bring out the best in a man. The wrong woman can bring out the worst, but you make Joshua shine."

Stella blinked. "Really?"

"Like a new penny," Olivia chortled.

Isobel skipped up to them, her brow wrinkling. "Uncle Joshua doesn't look like a penny."

The two women laughed. "He does on the inside," Stella stated, ruffling her hair.

Isobel continued to frown but didn't ask anything further.

"I look forward to calling you sister," Olivia said a moment later.

Stella's eyes widened, her lips parting as she held Olivia's gaze. She'd never had a sister, but then, neither had Olivia. Her eyes glistened and Stella murmured a thank you.

"I always wanted sisters when I was little," Olivia continued. "Now, I'm all grown up and have children of my own, and suddenly I've got three. You, Serena, and Janella. God works in mysterious ways."

"He does, doesn't He?"

Olivia nodded. "You've given my brother back to us. That means more to me than you can ever imagine, especially after losing Julian. I thought we'd lost Joshua a long time ago, and after Julian's death, he'd be gone completely. But he's still here. At least for now." She paused. "Once you two marry, things may change and you might want to start out on your own."

"I don't think so. Goddard Downs is our home. Where else would we go?"

Olivia shrugged. "We'll see. Let's grab a coffee and clean these kids up."

CHAPTER 23

$\mathcal{T}$he first weekend retreat was deemed a success, and more were planned. However, with the children gone, the focus turned to the wedding preparations.

Janella had joined most of the family on a trip to Darwin to shop for new clothes and other bits and pieces. It was a rare time when so many of them were off the station at the same time, but Nathan and David had offered to stay behind and were managing things with the help of the hands. It was a whirlwind trip, just three days, but long enough for them to find what they needed and get back home.

Janella's reasons for going to the city were far from trousseaus and suits. She was there to see her son. It felt like a lifetime since she'd last been with Caleb, although it had only been a few months. She missed him so much and couldn't wait to see him.

Approaching the main building, she scanned the groups of

students she passed, but he wasn't amongst them, so she headed to the reception desk.

A man of about fifty sat behind it and looked up. His nice smile helped ease her anxiety.

"Hello," she said. "I'm here to see Caleb Goddard."

"You're his mother?"

She nodded. She'd phoned ahead to say she was coming.

"One moment." He picked up the phone while scanning a list stuck to the top of his desk. After a few moments, he spoke into the receiver, "Caleb, your mother's here to see you." He nodded, hung up, and then told Janella that Caleb was on his way.

She hovered near the desk while she waited. The reception area was cavernous. She remembered it from when she'd brought Caleb to the school just a few months ago. It had seemed just as imposing then, with its vaulted ceiling and tiled floor that made the room echo.

"Your son's a fine young man, Mrs. Goddard," the man said.

"Thank you."

"He's very polite. Children nowadays don't seem to mind their manners or respect their elders, but he does. You've done a mighty job."

Her heart swelled with pride. Not for her, but for Caleb. Having a stranger speak so highly of her son made her prouder than ever. "We did our best."

The man nodded towards the steps. "Here he comes."

Janella followed the direction of his nod. Caleb looked so dashing in his uniform. He bounded down the staircase towards her. "Mum!"

Tears pricked her eyes. "Caleb," she said as he ran into her embrace. She kissed both of his cheeks before she caught herself. "Sorry. You're a big boy now and I'm sure you don't want your mother kissing you in public."

He grinned and hugged her tighter. "I missed you."

"Not as much as I've missed you. Let me get a good look at you." She took a step back and cast her gaze over him. He'd grown an inch taller already, she was sure of it. And he'd filled out.

"I didn't think I'd see you before I came home for Uncle Josh's wedding."

"The others were coming to Darwin to shop for clothes, so I came along. I wanted to see you."

"I can't believe he's getting married."

Janella chuckled. "Nor can I, but I'm happy about it. Stella's good for him."

"I think so too," Caleb agreed, sounding very mature. "I like her. She's smart and fun."

Janella smiled as they strolled out the main door and into the warm sunlight. The day was glorious, and she was very glad she'd made the long trip. "How are you liking it here? Is everything going well?"

He nodded. "I've made some friends. They're pretty cool. They love the same video games as me, and last year, one of the boys went to Russia with his parents. They're missionaries and his dad was sent there to do some work for their church."

"Russia? Wow! Have all the boys travelled? Do you feel bad that you haven't?"

Caleb shook his head. "No. They all want to come home with me. They've never been to a cattle station before and they want to see what it's like."

"Well, I'm sure we can figure something out. Serena had a group of students from town stay at the station last weekend. There was one boy, Jonah, who was a real help to me in the kitchen." She hugged Caleb to her side. "He reminded me of you."

"Really?"

"Yes. He's a little older, and a bit taller, but there was something about him that made me think of you. I suppose that's why I let him help me in the kitchen. His mum died a few years ago, and his dad hasn't done well ever since. The boy seemed a bit lost."

"That's sad. Maybe you can help him."

Janella frowned. "How could I do that?"

Caleb's face scrunched. "You're the best mum in the world and he doesn't have one. Maybe you could be there for him just like his mum would have been."

Janella was dumbfounded. Her son had left home as a boy but was already mature beyond his years. "Do you really think I could do that?"

"I know so. He's lost because he doesn't have a mother. If he had you or someone like you in his life, he'd do so much better."

"That's a very grown-up thing to say," Janella said, pride once again swelling within her.

"It makes sense, Mum. If I were a boy who didn't have a mother, I'd want you for my mum."

She smiled, pushing back the tears that were stinging her eyes. "Thank you, Caleb. That's a lovely thing to say."

"I mean it," he said, grinning.

Pulling him close, she gave him a tight hug. "Thank you. Hey, are you hungry?"

He laughed. "Always."

"Why don't we find something to eat? When do you have to be back?"

"I don't have any more classes today. There's a teachers' meeting for the next two periods, and then school's done for the day."

"That means I could take you out for lunch, and maybe dinner, too."

"We'll have to get a permission slip."

"Of course."

They returned to the main office area where Janella quickly filled out the form. Within moments, Caleb's leave was approved, but before venturing out, they went to his room so he could get changed. Janella smiled to see a picture of the entire family stuck to the side of his small wardrobe.

As they headed out, she glanced at her son and grinned. *There was no doubt that Julian would be proud of his son.*

"JANELLA WAS HAVING A GOOD TIME TONIGHT," Frank said as he took hold of Maggie's hand and kissed it gently.

"Yes, she did seem to be having fun. It's the first time in a long time."

"Let's hope it's not the last."

Maggie nodded in agreement.

"I'm glad we could steal away," Frank commented as they strolled along the wharf, leaving Pearls, their favourite restaurant, behind. The rest of the family group was still there, enjoying what remained of their meal.

"It seems that every time we come back here it's because something is about to change in our lives," Maggie said. "Our first date. When you proposed, and now with Joshua and Stella getting married."

Frank nodded. "This place seems to mark good things in our lives." Maggie's observation was accurate, as always. He was glad they had someplace special where they could celebrate these special milestones. Although tonight it was shared with their family, it still felt like just theirs.

"The next trip we take has to be our holiday back to Broome."

"Oh yes," Maggie said, smiling. "I'm so looking forward to returning to the sun and the sand and seeing you in your swim trunks." She grinned.

Stopping, Frank turned and gazed into her eyes. "Have I told you today how much I love you?"

Maggie chuckled. "Not yet."

"How remiss of me," he said, gently pressing his lips to hers. "I love you, Maggie Goddard."

"And I love you, Frank Goddard." She smiled as she kissed him back.

He slipped his arm across her shoulders and they continued their stroll. Only a slice of the moon was out, and the sky sparkled with a swathe of stars.

"It's beautiful," Maggie said, leaning into him.

He nodded. "It definitely is."

They made their way to 'their bench' and took a seat. Maggie nestled closer, resting her head on his shoulder as they gazed across the water.

He rubbed her arm. "What's this I'm hearing about the hens' and bucks' night?"

"Oh, Joshua and Stella have decided to forgo separate events and do one big party two days before the wedding, at a restaurant in Kununurra, or at the station. They haven't quite decided."

He frowned. "Why haven't they? Isn't having it two days before the wedding a bit too much? And if they want to have it at home, shouldn't Janella be preparing for it by now?"

Maggie threw her head back and laughed and then squeezed his hand. "If it was any earlier, Stella's family wouldn't be here. It's a long drive from Kununurra back home, and they need all the time they can get to prepare for the big day and make sure everyone's rested, so having it at home makes the most sense. Although it'll mean extra work for us, expenses will be kept down. And there's still plenty of time to shop. I'll help Janella, but Elizabeth has been amazing. She's a born organiser, and she and Janella will pull it together, I'm sure."

Frank smiled. No matter how many times he heard Maggie call Goddard Downs home, it still didn't feel real. It felt like just yesterday that he'd proposed. And it felt like a dream that she'd married him at all. But their marriage and life together *was* real. And he was the most blessed of men to call her his wife.

"They'll need to send out invitations soon," Maggie added, drawing Frank away from his thoughts.

"They should, if they want anyone to come."

"Don't worry. Everything's in hand, although there's a lot to do when planning a wedding, but Serena, Olivia, Janella, Elizabeth and I will make sure it all comes off without a hitch."

He pulled Maggie close and hugged her tight. "Thank you for being so wonderful, and for taking such a big part in all of this."

She smiled. "Joshua might not be my son by blood, but he's my son at heart, and this wedding has allowed us to grow closer and for me to feel more of a mother to him. I'm grateful to be able to help and am honoured to be part of this wonderful work of God."

Frank stroked her arm with his hand as he stared across the water. "God does so much that we don't understand. Months ago, we were lamenting Julian's death. Today, we're celebrating the coming union of two people under God's greatest covenant." He released a long breath and faced her. "I'm glad you've been with me through it all, my love. I don't know how I would have made it if you hadn't been by my side, praying, reminding me that God sees the big picture and that no matter what, He's in control."

He tipped her chin with his finger and gazed into her eyes. Tears glistened in them as he lowered his mouth and brushed his lips against hers. He'd thought that loving Esther meant he could never love another. He was so thankful to have been wrong. God had brought two wonderful women into his life. He was truly blessed.

CHAPTER 24

Frank tapped his leg as he waited for the loan agent to call them in. Joshua sat beside him, his hands wringing together as he leaned over his knees, his elbows pressing into them. "What's taking so long? We had a three o'clock appointment," he grumbled.

"I think it's normal for appointments to run late, son," Frank said, although he was also impatient to hear whether the bank had finally approved their loan or not. "We just have to be patient."

Joshua released a big breath.

A few moments later, an older man with a balding patch and spectacles poked his head around the door and waved them over. "Sorry, I got held up, Frank, Joshua. Good to see you both." He extended his hand and shook theirs in turn.

"It's not a problem, Cam. We understand," Frank said. The man had been in constant contact with them over the past months as they'd negotiated the loan and the proposed purchase of Indigo, and he'd become a firm friend.

"Take a seat." He waved to the chairs on the opposite side of the desk as he eased his large frame into a leather armchair. A ficus plant filled one corner of the room, providing some colour to the otherwise stark walls. A computer sat in the bend of his L-shaped desk. Trays of papers marked 'received', 'approved', and 'pending' sat on the right. The Goddard file was on top of the pending tray.

Frank took a long breath and uttered one final prayer. So much hung on this deal. Somehow, they'd been able to keep it from Stella. As expected, she'd dismissed the idea of running extra head of cattle on Goddard Downs and believed the deal was off the table. She had no idea they were planning on buying Indigo. Just as well, because it wasn't a done deal. Yet.

Joshua's heel tapped the floor as they waited for the final answer. He was more anxious than Frank. While this was simply a business deal to him, it was Joshua's life, his future with Stella.

Frank placed a hand on his knee. "Stop," he whispered. The tapping ceased.

Cam leaned forward, folding his arms on the desk. A small grin appeared on his face. "I won't keep you in suspense any longer. Your loan's approved."

Frank exhaled the breath he'd been holding, while Joshua clapped a hand on Frank's shoulder and shook his arm so vigorously that Frank thought it might wrench out of its socket. "We got it, Dad! Stella's going to go crazy when she finds out. I can't wait to tell her. This is going to be the best wedding present ever."

Looking at his son's smiling face, Frank couldn't help but feel joy and sorrow. His son's happiness meant he'd be leaving his side, possibly for good. Though Indigo wasn't far away, it was far enough. But it felt right that he and Stella start their married life without the shadows of the past holding them back. "Yes, she will be," he said.

"I'm happy we were able to oblige you in the end. I'm only sorry it took so long," Cam said.

Frank shrugged. "It's okay. Everything in God's time. And we were able to push out the timeframe with Ravi Tamala, so all's well." Ravi had been surprisingly understanding and had kept the deal on the table, despite it taking much longer than originally expected to get an answer. "So, what's next?"

"A ton of paperwork. If you've got the time, we can make a start now."

"We've got the time if you have," Frank said.

"Righteo." Cam opened their file and pulled out a wad of paperwork about an inch thick. "I'll explain these to you as best I can, but you should go through them with a lawyer before signing them."

Frank had figured as much. Confident that the loan would be approved, he'd set up a tentative appointment with their lawyer for four o'clock.

Cam quickly explained the terms of the loan, and then placed the paperwork into a large envelope which he handed to Frank. "Get them back to me as soon as you can."

Frank took the envelope and he and Joshua stood. "Thanks. We might even get them back to you today."

"Great. Oh, and Joshua…"

"Yes?" Joshua angled his head.

"All the best for your wedding. I hear it's soon." Extending his hand, he smiled.

"Yes, it is. Three weeks and counting." Beaming, Joshua shook Cam's hand. "Thank you."

Cam nodded. "You're welcome."

Frank and Joshua left the office and walked out of the bank, heads high and spirits soaring. It was happening. They were about to become the owners of Indigo Downs. At least for a while, until Joshua handed over the deed to Stella as a wedding gift.

"This has to be the best day of my life," Joshua said as they walked the three blocks to the lawyer's office. "I can't wait to see Stella's face."

"I know," Frank replied. "But be patient. Your wedding day will be here before you know it."

They rounded a corner, and as they passed the door of a bar, out stumbled a familiar face. "Sean?" Frank blinked. He couldn't believe it.

"Uncle Frank?" Sean staggered to a halt and stared at him before swinging his unsteady gaze to Joshua. "Josh?"

Joshua drew a long breath. "Sean."

"It's been a while, Sean. How've you been?" Frank asked, although by the smell of the alcohol on his breath, Frank already knew.

"Fine," Sean replied, his gaze still on Joshua. He raised his chin slightly. "How are things?"

"Good," Joshua answered. "I'm getting married."

Sean scoffed. "You're making a mistake. You know that."

"I'm not. It's the best choice I've ever made."

Sean smacked his lips and backed away. "Well, it's been nice seeing you both. I've got some fun to have. I'll be seeing you."

Joshua went to follow him but stopped. Frank knew how hard it must be for him to see his cousin in such a state. They'd been so close for so long. "He's making his own choices, son."

"I wish he'd make better ones," Joshua mumbled.

Frank patted him on the back. "He'll come around one day. Mark my words."

"I'm not so sure about that. He's livid about me getting married."

"I think he's envious. Anyway, he's a grown man, and we have paperwork to sign."

Joshua blew out another breath. "Yes, you're right."

"We'll keep him in our prayers. That's all we can do."

Joshua nodded as they continued along the street. No doubt seeing Sean had taken the shine off the loan approval, but only momentarily. As soon as they sat down with the lawyer, the reality that Indigo Downs would soon be theirs would be as real as the light of day.

CHAPTER 25

*J*oshua and Stella's wedding was less than two weeks away, but something else played on Janella's mind. Caleb's words echoed in her head, confirmation of the voice that whispered in her heart. *Help Jonah. He needs someone to believe in him.* He needs *you* to believe in him. No matter how she tried, she couldn't shake the voice. She told herself it wasn't her place. He had teachers, and it was Serena, not her, who was heading up the program. She should be the last person to intercede. Regardless, the voice kept whispering, tugging her heart, until she had no choice but to make the trip she was now taking.

Since she didn't go into town very often on her own, she hoped no one would quiz her about what she was doing there, or offer to go with her, because she guessed they might try to stop her if they knew. She'd do some shopping for the bucks' and hens' party while there, so at least she could use that as a legitimate excuse. But no one quizzed her, although Frank was a little concerned about her driving there and back on her own.

She started the engine and headed down the track. The landscape took on a new beauty as she drove through the harsh terrain. Bauhinia clustered near a mound of large rocks. The shrub wasn't the prettiest, but it was quite useful. Her ancestors used the nectar and gum, which was sweet, for food, while the bark was used for treating headaches and fever. It burned well and was good for firewood. Towering boab trees, with their thick trunks, stood like pot-bellied sentinels watching over the land. She remembered climbing them as a child when she and Julian would go exploring between his classes at the school of the air. She hadn't attended school as he did. Her lessons had been different, but nonetheless valuable. Before her family came to Goddard Downs, she'd gone to a school where she not only learned to read and write, but about the heritage of her people. Caleb and Sasha didn't have that kind of education, but she'd taught them what they needed to know. They were fortunate to have parents from different backgrounds. The differences between her and Julian made for a richer life for their children.

Slowly the terrain changed, and with it Janella's mood. The calm she felt soon turned to anxiety as the open plains gave way to buildings and homes, and the roads which had been quiet, teemed with noisy traffic. She could never be a town-dweller. The noise and busyness would steal her peace, and that was something she wasn't willing to give up.

And youth crime was on the rise. Only two months earlier, a terrible incident in Kununurra had left the townsfolk shaken.

An indigenous youth, high on drugs and alcohol, raped and killed a teenage girl.

Things had to change. Serena's program was a step in the right direction, but for many, it had come too late.

The question burned in Janella's heart. *Was it too late to help Jonah?* She prayed not. The boy needed help. *Her* help, and she was going to give it. She was determined. Caleb was right, Jonah needed a mother figure to believe in him, but first, she had to speak with his father.

She'd gotten Jonah's address from the school counsellor. The woman questioned her motives at first, but after Janella assured her that she only wanted to help, and that she worked alongside Serena, the woman conceded and divulged the address.

After referring to her directions several times, she finally found the street. The area was rundown. Gutted cars piled on empty lots, broken bottles and rubbish littered the footpath, and graffiti covered the walls of vacant buildings. There wasn't a hint of green anywhere, and the air reeked of tobacco and something else as she drove past a group of young men playing dice on the corner. Looking into their eyes, she saw emptiness. Lives devoid of hope. Her heart cried for them. *Lord, I pray one day they'll find their way. That they'll know what it is to live, not just exist. Draw them to Yourself, Lord. Give them hope. Give them life.*

Janella almost changed her mind as she parked the jeep outside the small blue house with a broken front window. Instead of grass, the front yard was filled with dirt and straggly weeds. An old rusty car stacked on bricks sat in the driveway. There was no sign of wheels anywhere. She'd come this far, so she couldn't turn back now. She locked the car door and walked toward the driveway, glancing in both directions to see if anyone on the street was taking note of her. The boys she'd passed seemed more preoccupied with their dice than her, and no one else was about. *Perhaps she should have asked Frank or Joshua to come with her.*

But she'd wanted to make this trip alone since she didn't want to embarrass Jonah. It was one thing to have someone come to your house unexpected and offer help, but it was another when they brought people with them you weren't close to. It made it feel more like charity and not kindness. It became a spectacle, and the last thing Janella wanted was for Jonah or his father to feel apprehensive about what she was offering.

Heart pounding, she walked carefully up the two rotting steps onto the porch and knocked on the door. There was no response. She waited, fidgeting with her hands and glancing up and down the street to see if anyone was watching. It wasn't the safest place, and if Julian were alive, he'd be upset to know she was there alone.

After several seconds, she knocked again. "Hello! Anyone home?"

"Quit your shouting! People are trying to sleep," a male voice responded from inside.

Janella stepped back at the sound of movement and a hissed curse. A man, dressed in striped boxers and a buttoned-down shirt he hadn't bothered to fasten, opened the door a moment later. His frame was gaunt, his hair shaggy and greasy, and he reeked of stale alcohol. He looked her over. "I don't want whatever it is you're selling. Off you go."

He tried to close the door, but Janella stuck her foot in it. "I'm not selling anything. I'm here about your son, Jonah."

He eyed her suspiciously. "What about Jonah?"

She cleared her throat. "Mr. Barambah, my name's Janella Goddard. I work at Goddard Downs, the cattle station in the Kimberley where Jonah's been going on weekends."

"So?"

"I'd like a moment to speak with you if you have some time."

He groaned. "What did he do? He did something, didn't he? I knew that boy would only get himself in trouble. I knew it."

"No, sir. Jonah hasn't done anything wrong. He's been nothing but a huge help to me."

His brow wrinkled into deep creases that changed his features completely, making him look ten years older. She wasn't sure that it was concern for Jonah that aged him, or the harshness of his life. "Then why are you here?"

She sighed. "Could we speak inside? This matter won't take long, but it's one I'd rather discuss away from the ears of others." She met his gaze and held it. Again, she saw hopelessness in the eyes staring back at her.

He stepped aside. "Come in." His voice was gruff and not the least bit friendly or welcoming.

"Thank you." Janella gave a small smile.

The house was small but appeared even smaller due to the many dark corners. There was a smell of mildew, and the air was thick, as if the windows hadn't been opened in years. By the looks of the dust on them, it might very well have been that long.

"This way," he said, pointing to a small sitting room to the left. "Give me a minute to make myself presentable."

Janella gave a nod and headed for the room. The carpet was old, matted, and heavily stained. She didn't want to think what from. The couch was green and reminded her of the moss found on the base of trees. She stepped towards it and part of her cringed, but she forced herself to sit. There was a single chair across from it, but she felt better about the couch than the piece of brown furniture. She didn't want to make Jonah's father feel uncomfortable, as if she was shunning his home. Still, she kept her arms, and bag, close to her body while she perched on the edge of the seat and wondered at the wisdom of entering the house in the first place. He seemed harmless enough, but Julian would have been horrified that she was there at all.

When he returned, Mr. Barambah looked moderately better. He was now wearing pants, for which she was thankful, and the shirt was buttoned and tucked in. His hair was slicked back against his head, the unruly ends sticking up in places. He took a seat in the chair across from her. "So, you said you're here about Jonah."

"Yes, I am." She swallowed her anxiety. *Lord, give me strength.* "I wanted to speak to you about his future."

She didn't expect her declaration to elicit a laugh, but it did. "What future?"

"You've thought about what Jonah's going to do once he leaves the community school, haven't you?"

He shook his head. "Nuh. Haven't given it a thought."

"Well, I have."

His eyes narrowed.

She swallowed hard. "I think your son's very talented. He's been helping me in the kitchen, and he has a natural talent, something he says he learned from his mother."

He stiffened slightly and glanced away.

"Jonah told me you lost your wife some years ago. I'm sorry."

He swung his gaze back to her. "What does that have to do with you? You didn't know us. Why should you be sorry? Did you make her sick? Did you let her die?"

Grief and despair made him talk that way, so she didn't react. Instead, she continued with what she'd come to say and hoped that by sharing some of her own grief, he'd be open to her proposal.

"I know how difficult it is to lose the person you love. My husband died less than a year ago. It still feels like yesterday. I have two children. Caleb and Sasha. They mean the world to me, as I am sure Jonah means to you. If anything were to happen to me, I'd want someone to help them."

"Is that why you're here?" Mr. Barambah sprang to his feet. "We don't need help. We're doing just fine."

Janella remained seated. "With all due respect, I don't think so."

"What do you know about it? You come here to judge the way we live?"

"Not at all. I came here because your son came to me. He saw something in me that he needed, and I'm here because I'm willing to give him that."

"What does he need from you?"

"Someone to believe in him."

Her words seemed to hit home. He stared at her, the lump in his throat bobbing.

"Your son can be great. I know it. I believe it. I have faith that he could do wonderful things, but he needs help. That's why I came to you. As his father, I know you'd only want the best for him. I also thought it preferable to gain your approval before I went ahead. But, whether you agree or refuse, I intend to help your son, one way or another."

"Then why come at all?"

"Because it would mean the world to Jonah if you supported him. If you were the one to encourage him in his pursuits."

"What pursuits?" His brows came together and she could almost see his mind ticking over.

"Culinary school." Her heart raced. She was relieved he hadn't turned her out of the house yet. She'd been brazen, but she had to keep going. She had to say all she'd come to say. She didn't know where the boldness was coming from, or the words. She hadn't a clue what she would say before he opened the door, but now the words flowed out of her, and she prayed that each one hit the mark.

Mr. Barambah lowered himself into his seat. "Culinary school is expensive."

"It can be. But there are scholarships and grants he can apply for. I can also lend a hand if you'd let me."

He eyed her sceptically. "Why're you doing this?"

She smiled. "Because the day I met your son, I saw my own. I thought of how I'd feel if Caleb lost me and didn't know how to find his way. Then I spoke to my son. He told me that I should help Jonah. That he needs a mother figure in his life, and that I was the right person to help in that department."

"Jonah had a mother." His voice softened. "He doesn't need another."

"He needs someone to love him as a mother does. In the weeks since he started coming to Goddard Downs, I've grown to love your son like my own. He has such a quiet spirit, but he hides so much behind bravado, trying to seem tough and strong, while inside, he's scared and lonely. He's still grieving," Janella continued. "You both are."

Mr. Barambah blew out a breath and gazed out the filthy window. "When my wife was alive, everything was great. She made sure of it. That boy couldn't leave this house with a wrinkle in his clothes or a hair out of place. My Miriam was a great mother. There was no one like her." His gaze narrowed on Janella. "No one."

"I'm not trying to replace her. I just want to be there for Jonah. Please, Mr. Barambah, I need your help. Your son needs your help. He needs you to believe in him. He needs you to come back from where you are and be his father again."

He bristled, but she pushed on. "Please, hear me out. I don't mean to offend, and I'm certainly not here to judge. I just see a family in need of help. You're both still feeling the hollowness of loss, the pain of knowing you'll never see your Miriam again, but Jonah needs you, Mr. Barambah."

She didn't expect what happened next. A sniffle broke the dam and the man across from her, who seemed so gruff and belligerent, began to weep. "Don't you think I know? I'm no good for my son. It kills me. I don't know what to do. Where to start."

Janella swallowed hard, unsure of what to do.

Therefore encourage one another and build each other up, just as in fact you are doing.

She took a deep breath. "You can start by allowing me to help. I know you don't want things to be this way. I know you want what's best for Jonah, and yourself. You've lost your way, but you can find it again. You just have to make a start."

She stood and walked towards him, stretching out her hand. "Let me partner with you. I believe we can make a difference if we work together. I truly do. You don't know me, and you have no reason to believe or trust me, but I'm asking you. Begging you. Let me be a friend to you both."

He gazed at her hand as if it would sprout teeth and bite, but slowly, the apprehension melted away. He stood and took her hand. "You really believe you can help my boy? Turn things around for him?"

She smiled. "For both of you, if you let me."

Tears welled in his eyes and he nodded.

Janella's heart leaped inside her. "That's wonderful. I brought some things for you to look over. We can go through them now if you'd like, or I can leave them with you and come back another time."

"We can look at them now. Jonah's out and he won't be back for a while."

"Good. I want him to think this came from you more than from me. Shall we start?" she asked eagerly.

He nodded. "Fire away."

CHAPTER 26

*T*he lawn at Goddard Downs was filled with bucks and hens. Not the feathered variety. The human variety, all raring to have a good time before Joshua and Stella tied the knot. Work on the station had been suspended in the days before to ensure everything was ready for the party. Every eco-hut and guest accommodation was packed with party goers. Maggie was working double time in the kitchen with Janella, Sasha and Jonah, to make sure everyone was fed and watered. It was a bit hectic, but she was enjoying herself. Even now, as she stood julienning vegetables, she was humming a favourite tune in her head.

"Two days. Can you believe it's just two days until the wedding?" she asked Janella as she popped a carrot stick in her mouth. The vegetable crunched loudly in her ears and tasted so sweet. "These are a good bunch."

"Yes. The vegetables have done well this year," Janella replied. "And yes, it's hard to believe Joshua will be married so soon. It seems like yesterday he was still this lost man trying to find his way. Despite my initial misgivings about the marriage, he's grown into a responsible man." She sighed thoughtfully. "If only Julian could've seen it. It's all he ever wanted for his brother."

Maggie let out a deep breath and smiled sympathetically. She knew how hard it still was for Janella to accept that Julian was gone. "He would have been proud."

"Yes, he would have been," Janella said, nodding.

"Where do you want these, Janella?" Jonah interrupted. He had a tray of freshly washed blueberries in his hand. His hair was pulled back in a short ponytail revealing his handsome features.

"You should wear your hair like that more often," Maggie said, smiling. "It shows how handsome you are."

Janella nodded. "I agree. And you can put the blueberries next to the strawberries, and then get to squeezing lemons."

Jonah acted without question. His focus and commitment was inspiring. Of all the children who'd come to Goddard Downs, he showed the most potential. Though the project was Serena's idea, Maggie believed it was God-inspired, and because of it, Jonah had found the help he needed. Serena wasn't the door to him moving forward. Janella was, and Maggie could already see the change in her. Her spark had returned, praise God. She leaned closer to her friend. "He's a good boy."

"That he is." Janella beamed as she glanced his way. "And he and Caleb get along so well. I was a little anxious when they met, but it's like they've known each other all their lives.

They've bonded over some computer game where the characters do whacky dances."

Maggie chuckled. "I'm glad. And how does Sasha like him?"
She lowered her voice. Sasha was focused on decorating a fruit
flan, but Maggie didn't want her to hear them talking
about her.

"The same," Janella replied, glancing at her daughter. "They
talk about recipes mostly. Boys and girls at their age can be a
bit awkward together, and Sasha has her friends and interests
and so does Jonah, so they don't talk much outside of food-
making."

A roar of laughter drifted in from the outside. "Sounds like
the Martin clan are having a grand time." Maggie peered out
the window to see what they were laughing at.

"Sounds like it. They're quite the bunch." Janella chuckled.

"Not quite what I expected knowing Stella, but nice people
all the same."

"They're what you'd call eccentric," Janella said as she added
some herbs to the bolognaise she was making.

Stella's family outnumbered the Goddards two-to-one.
Some were loud and boisterous, others so reserved they hardly
spoke. Maggie knew from conversations that they all didn't
share Stella's beliefs, but they weren't judgmental about it. They
loved her and were there to support her, even if they didn't
entirely understand the rush to wed. Some didn't think
marriage was necessary at all, but that was another matter. Since
their arrival two days before, Maggie had taken the opportunity
to get to know them, as did the rest of the family. After all, they
were about to become connected for the rest of their lives.

"I can see why Stella wanted an intimate ceremony," Janella commented. She stirred the kangaroo bolognaise. Before moving to Goddard Downs, Maggie hadn't tasted kangaroo, but it was as tasty as beef and gave the dish a twist. Janella was a master of concocting recipes that turned out great every time.

"Yes," Maggie agreed. "What with her large family, everyone here on the station, plus their friends from all over, there were far too many people for them to invite any others. I hope no one was offended they didn't get invited to the wedding."

"What does it matter?" Janella shrugged. "They'll get over it. If they don't, then Stella and Josh will know who truly cares about them. When Julian and I married, we didn't have a huge wedding. Some people took offense and refused to speak to us after, but we took that as God eliminating those who couldn't help us on the next stage of our lives."

Maggie smiled. "Well said."

"Janella," Jonah said hesitantly, as if he didn't want to interrupt.

She looked in his direction. "Yes, love."

"After the lemons, what do you want me to do?" He had a row of lemons lined up on the counter in front of him as he worked a hand juicer in his palms.

"One thing at a time, Jonah. You're always rushing ahead. When you're almost done with those, I'll let you know what's next." She chuckled and looked at Maggie. "Always ready to work. I love it," she whispered.

Maggie brought the crudité to where Janella stood and started arranging the tray. She leaned close and whispered. "How are things with the culinary school applications?"

Janella glanced over her shoulder before answering. "Great. It took a little convincing, but once he realised that his father and I were behind him, he was willing to try. I plan to take some photos of the desserts he's made for tonight and add them to his portfolio."

"Portfolio?" Maggie's brows scrunched. She'd heard of portfolios for art, design, and even writing. She had one herself, but for food?

"Yes, cooking isn't simply cooking, it's art. Having a portfolio will help him not only have something to show the admission boards of the schools, and hopefully make up for what he might lack in grades, but he can continue to add to it as he learns more and improves. Later, it can make a big impression when showing a prospective employer."

Maggie marvelled. "How do you know all this?"

Janella chuckled. "I was doing some reading and came across an article. You know I like to look at new recipes to inspire me with my own. Well, there was an article on *Food Magazine's* website, and I read it."

Maggie laughed. "There's so much more to you than meets the eye, Janella. Have you ever considered going to culinary school yourself? You'd be amazing."

"Not me. I'm too old. Besides, I have too much to do here."

"That's not true," Maggie protested. "Age doesn't matter, or did you miss that memo? You can do anything you want at any age. Moses was eighty when he went before Pharaoh to free the Israelites. And he believed he lacked the skill to speak and do the job, but we know how that ended. You have a God-given gift to be a great chef."

Janella chuckled and shook her head. "I don't think so."

"I mean it. I'm sure there's a school somewhere that would take you."

"Yes, Janella," Jonah interjected.

Maggie hadn't noticed when he'd started listening, but as the conversation changed, they'd become a little more comfortable and less discrete.

"You don't know what you're saying, Jonah. Culinary school is for you. Not me," Janella replied.

"Why not both of us? You can apply with me. We could even end up at the same school," he said brightly.

"It's true." Maggie nodded and turned more to her friend. "If you wanted to do it, Frank would understand. We could manage while you were off studying. I'm sure it wouldn't be a problem. I could step in to help, and Olivia knows how to cook."

Janella laughed. "Maybe, but right now, we have a hens' and bucks' party to cater for. Back to work. Jonah. When you're done, you can start working on your chocolate surprise tarts."

"Yes!" the boy said, pumping his fist.

Maggie and Janella laughed together. The evening was already turning out wonderfully, and the fun had only just begun.

Lord, let this night be one of many to remember. May it be filled with love, joy, and peace. Father, I ask that You give inspiration to Janella and Jonah. Show them their full potential. Help them to see all that they can be, and allow them to live without limits. Bless Joshua and Stella as they prepare to take these first steps into matrimony. May Your hand be upon them, and may Your grace surround them. In Jesus' name. Amen.

JOSHUA STOOD SIPPING his soda and laughing with Stella's cousin, Ned. He was an insurance agent from Cootamundra who moonlighted as a stand-up comedian. He was quite good. At least Joshua found him funny.

"Then the Rabbi says," Ned stated, but Joshua missed the punchline. He'd picked up something in his periphery, a gait he hadn't seen at Goddard Downs in a very long time. "Sean," he whispered under his breath. He turned to Ned and patted him on the arm. "Excuse me a moment, will you?"

"Sure. Sure. Do what you have to. I'll be here," the other man replied with a chuckle.

Joshua's heart raced as he peered through the crowd. Sean hovered on the outskirts, far enough not to be a part of the festivities, but close enough to be seen. Joshua wove his way through the crowd, short-cutting through the makeshift dance floor. The real one would be installed on the morning of the wedding.

Although Sean had been so against the marriage, Joshua had sent an invitation anyway, but he hadn't expected him to come. But here he was. Joshua prayed he wasn't there to cause trouble.

His steps quickened.

His cousin was dressed in a simple white t-shirt and jeans. His arm was in a cast. *What had he done now?*

"Sean. I didn't know you were coming." He was breathless by the time he reached him.

Sean shrugged, grinning. "Couldn't miss this shindig."

Joshua raised a brow. "Thought you were against me getting married."

Sean shrugged again. "Yeah, well. You're my cuz. How could I miss it?"

Joshua blew out a breath. "What're you really saying, Sean?"

His cousin lifted his head slowly and met his gaze. "I've been a jerk, okay? I admit it." He kicked at the grass with his boot. "I didn't want you to get with Stella. I knew that if you did, everything would change, and it did. You stopped living the way we wanted to. The way *I* wanted to. I knew you'd change because you were never really about that life. I knew it, and I knew that having her in your life would make you see it."

He was right. Stella *had* made him realise that he didn't want that kind of reckless life anymore. He nodded.

"That's why I thought it was a mistake. I knew it would change everything between us, that we'd no longer be able to do the things I wanted. To have the life I wanted to live. You'd leave me behind like everyone else did. You'd forget me."

The look of despondency in Sean's eyes rendered Joshua speechless. All he could do was stand and listen as his cousin poured out his heart, as he'd never heard him do before.

"I'm not the smartest guy. I could never be a success at anything but riding bulls, and without you there to support me, even that seemed impossible. Everyone sees me as a waste. You were the only one who didn't. I didn't want to lose that. But that was selfish. I see that now."

"Sean…"

"Hear me out. I wanted to keep you and Stella apart so I could have my dreams. I never once considered what you wanted. I was happy as long as we were on the same page. I lied to myself that you'd be happy doing whatever made me happy. I didn't think of you. I'm sorry."

"It's okay, mate. No harm done." Joshua gave a smile he hoped conveyed his forgiveness.

"I know it might be too late to say this, but I had to. I couldn't let you get married hating me."

Joshua stepped forward and clapped a gentle hand on Sean's shoulder. "I never hated you. I love you, mate. I just wanted you to be happy for me. I wanted *you* to be happy."

Sean's eyes glistened. "Don't get all mushy on me, Josh. You know I'm not a sappy fella."

Joshua laughed. "Mushy? You're the one who drove three hours to get here to say this. Doesn't that count as some level of mushiness? At least sentimentality."

"Not at all. It's called owning up to your mistakes." Though his tone was serious, there was a hint of a laugh in it. A bit of the Sean that Joshua was used to seeing.

"So, how'd you come by a broken arm?"

Sean glanced down at his arm and laughed. "The last bull I rode was craftier than I thought. He bucked me right off in less than five seconds. I fell on my arm and broke it in two places. I've got two pins in there now."

"You had surgery? Why didn't you call? I would've come," Joshua said, shocked.

Sean shrugged. "I didn't think you would."

"Of course I would have. You're my cousin, Sean. We've always been there for each other."

"Not recently. But that's my fault."

"So, what are you going to do with yourself now? How're you getting by?"

Sean shrugged. "Not sure. I'll figure something out."

"Are you working?"

He shook his head.

Joshua's mind ticked over. "We've got a new hand, David, Serena's husband, but there's always room for another. The more there are, the lighter the load."

"The way I left before, I don't think I'd be welcome. I think that was one time too many," Sean replied.

Joshua squeezed his shoulder. "You might be surprised. The Bible says to forgive seventy times seven."

"That's right." Joshua turned. His dad had appeared out of nowhere. "And at Goddard Downs, we practice what we preach."

Sean blinked. "Uncle Frank."

"Sean. Good to see you," he said smiling. "I'm sorry to intrude, but I couldn't help but overhear."

"You were listening, Dad?"

"I was. And I'm glad." He turned to Sean. "I won't pretend that I was pleased with how you left here. However, knowing you and Joshua as I do, I knew there was something more to it. Having heard your discussion just now, I understand even better."

"I'm very sorry, Uncle. I know I don't deserve your forgiveness. And I'm not going to ask for it."

Frank smiled. "None of us deserve forgiveness, but God gives it freely. If He can forgive, then we must, too."

Sean's face crumpled. "You mean that? You'd forgive me?"

"I already have, Sean."

"You see," Joshua said with a laugh, patting his cousin on

the back. "You're welcome. Why don't you come and join the party?"

Sean shook his head. "I'm not dressed for it. Besides, you and Uncle Frank might have forgiven me, but there are people over there who won't be happy to see me. I'm sure they'll have something to say about me being here."

"No, they won't," his father rebutted. "And if they do, they'll have to speak to me."

Sean's eyes glistened again. "Thanks, Uncle Frank."

Frank patted Sean on the back and smiled. "Don't mention it. Go on. Enjoy the party. You were invited, and it's a relaxed affair. We'll be right behind you."

Joshua stood beside his father and smiled. "I'm surprised he came, but I'm glad."

"So am I."

Joshua folded his arms over his chest contentedly.

"Josh?"

"Yes, Dad."

"Did I hear correctly that you offered Sean a job here at Goddard Downs?"

He turned. "I did. I hope you don't mind. It just sort of popped out."

"Not at all. Sean's a good worker. If he needs employment, I'd be happy to help, but I think you forgot something."

Joshua sighed. "I know. We have to run it by the family."

"Not that. I'm sure they'll be fine. No, I mean you and Indigo. Did you forget that after the wedding, you and Stella won't be here anymore? Sean might not want to stay if he doesn't have you to support him."

How had he forgotten? "You're right. I didn't think of that."

"I didn't think so, but you'd better. Sean will be expecting you to be here." His father met his gaze, gave a nod, then walked back to the party.

Joshua stood silently as his father walked away. Sean was mingling with the family. Olivia and Nathan looked surprised, but they were smiling, so they seemed to be taking Sean's presence well. Joshua sought out Stella amongst the crowd. She was standing with Elizabeth, laughing. She was happy, and that was all that mattered. Whatever he said was done, and he wouldn't take it back. He breathed a sigh and headed back to the party.

There's a reason you brought him here, Lord. See it through.

CHAPTER 27

*I*t seemed like only yesterday they were in Darwin picking up items for the wedding. Now the big day was here. Maggie was so nervous it felt like her own wedding day, instead of Joshua and Stella's.

"Do you have your boutonniere?" she asked as she looked in the mirror to clip in her earrings. They were a lovely diamond starburst, a gift to herself during their trip to Darwin. She tucked her hair behind her ears, admiring the framing her new cut gave to her face.

"I left it on the counter in the kitchen," Frank called from the bathroom. Maggie could just hear him over the sound of his razor.

"Are you almost done?"

"Just about. You?"

"I'm ready," she replied, slipping her feet into her silver heels before retrieving the boutonniere from the kitchen. It was right where Frank said he'd left it.

Opening the container, she admired the flower as she carefully lifted it out. How Stella found someone who sold cornflower plants she would never know, but the girl was determined. She loved cornflowers. Maggie brushed the petals lightly. Other than the colour, the flower reminded her of a large marigold.

Frank walked into the room a moment later. She smelled his cologne before she heard his steps. He came up behind her and placed his hands on her shoulders and kissed her cheek. "You look gorgeous, my love."

Maggie smiled and turned in his arms, adoring the scent of him. "And you look very handsome." She took the flower, which already had a safety pin attached, and pinned it to his lapel.

Joshua had chosen casual wedding attire for himself and the groomsmen. Medium blue trousers, cornflower blue button-downs with the sleeves pushed up to the elbows, medium grey waistcoats, and matching suede shoes. Frank had chosen more formal attire, and he looked dashing in his dark suit.

He grinned and stole a kiss as she adjusted the pin. "We should get going."

She nodded. "Yes. I need to check on Stella and a few other things." Since there'd been several weddings in her family in recent years, including her own, and she knew the ropes, she'd taken the lead on the wedding planning. Stella's mother had been more than willing for her to take it on since she lived so far away, and now Gloria was enjoying some much needed quiet time with her daughter before she said her 'I do'.

Frank grabbed his keys and they headed out the door.

. . .

MUSIC RESOUNDED from the main house as they parked the car. A DJ had been hired for the day and was to start testing the sound system at twelve. Maggie checked her watch. "Right on time," she commented.

Frank glanced at the clock on the dash. "Good man. Let's hope everything else goes to plan."

She placed a hand on his thigh and smiled. "I'm sure it will. Are you okay, Frank?"

"Why wouldn't I be?"

"It's a big thing having your youngest fly the nest."

"He's more than ready. And I'm so proud of him."

"He's come such a long way in such a short time," she said.

"Yes. I'm excited to see what lies ahead for him and Stella."

"And I'm excited to see what lies ahead for you and me." She lifted her gaze and met his, grinning as he took her hand and kissed it.

"I love you, Maggie."

She smiled. "I never get tired of hearing that."

"I hope not. I plan on telling you for the rest of my life."

She smiled as warmth trickled through her body. They were so blessed to have each other. She inhaled deeply. It was going to be an amazing day. She could feel it.

"STELLA, sit for a while. You're making us all anxious," her mother said from her spot on the edge of the bed. Olivia and

Nathan had given up their bedroom for her to prepare in, since it was much larger than her own.

"I can't. I'm so nervous. Why am I so nervous?" she said in a voice too high to be her own.

"Calm yourself." Elizabeth stepped in front of her, blocking her path. She held Stella's hands and looked into her eyes. "Now, take a deep breath in through your nose and out through your mouth. Go on. Do it."

Stella mimicked the rhythmic action of her cousin's breathing.

"And again," Elizabeth said, puckering her lips as she blew out. They repeated the exercise until Stella's heart stopped racing and her mind became less frantic.

She smiled at Elizabeth and then laughed. "Thank you. I needed that."

"Don't mention it. I don't know what you're worried about. Everything's going to be perfect. Nothing's going to go wrong. Trust me."

Elizabeth and her perpetual optimism. "Is this another of those things you just know?"

Her cousin smiled. "Yup. Today will be a wonderful day. Now, let's get you dressed before time runs away." Elizabeth grabbed her hand and pulled her across the room.

Her dress hung in front of the window. The pale blue curtains seemed perfectly picked to match the colours for the day. The photographer had already been in there to take preliminary shots but would return soon to take the photos of her dressing. Stella stood and admired her dress.

"It really is lovely," Olivia commented from behind her.

"Yes," Janella agreed. She was standing on the other side of the room with Sasha, curling her daughter's hair with an iron.

"Thank you." Stella smiled. "Thank you all for being here."

"We have to welcome you into the family properly," Olivia replied. She was dressed in a calf-length, strapless dress which suited her tall, slender frame, and she looked totally glamorous.

A knock on the door announced the photographer's return, and soon they were arranging themselves in their different stages of undress so the makeup artist could save time with each of their faces, and the photographer could get her shots without wasting time.

"Sit here, Stella," Lucinda, the stylist, called. She patted the high back of the chair that sat in front of the vanity. Stella took a deep breath and sat, but she couldn't keep her eyes off of her dress which was still hanging in front of the window. It had a feel of whimsy to it, from the flowing material and uneven hemline that formed petal shapes around her ankles. The dress had spaghetti straps and a cornflower blue sash around the middle that hung down the back. The second she saw it in the store, she knew it was the one.

Lucinda was a miracle worker and soon Stella's hair was coiled in dozens of large curls and pinned back from her face with pearl-tipped beads. "She's ready," she said when the last pin was in place.

"Time for the dress," Elizabeth announced.

"I have it," Maggie said, smiling.

Stella hadn't even noticed Maggie arriving. "Hey, Maggie."

"Hi, Stella. Your hair looks lovely," she replied, taking the dress down from the window and bringing it over to her. "Here we go."

While Olivia, Janella and Sasha continued to get their hair and makeup done, Maggie, her mother, and Elizabeth helped her into her dress. She felt like a princess as they stood around her, adjusting it here and there until it was perfect. A tear stung her eyes as she thought how blessed she was to be supported by such an amazing group of women.

"Don't cry or you'll smudge your mascara," Elizabeth warned.

Lucinda laughed. "Waterproof, hon. Haven't you heard of it?"

"Fine," her cousin replied. "Still, red and blotchy doesn't look good for the photos."

"I don't get red and blotchy when I cry," Stella said.

"Not you, me. If you cry, you'll start me off, and I want to look good for the photos."

Everyone laughed.

When they were ready, Maggie called them together. "Ladies, if you would. I'd like you to circle Stella and hold hands."

"What are we doing?" Sasha asked.

"We're going to pray for Stella," Maggie said quietly as she took Sasha's hand in one of hers, and Gloria's in the other.

Stella glanced at her mother. She appreciated being prayed for, but what would her mother think?

There was no need to worry. Her mother gave a nod and then bowed her head as Maggie began to pray.

"Heavenly Father, we thank You for this day. We rejoice in it. We praise You for bringing Stella and Joshua together. You knew before the beginning of time the wonderful plans you have for these two young people, and we know that You'll be with them through all the years that lay ahead. God, richly bless them and make today the most memorable day of their lives. Grant them understanding, patience, and never-ending love, that they can stay side-by-side through every tide of life. Be their rock and their refuge. In Jesus' precious name. Amen."

"Amen," the other women chorused.

"Amen," Stella whispered as she slowly opened her eyes and smiled at Maggie. "Thank you," she said softly.

THERE WAS NOT a cloud in the sky as Stella stepped out of the house on her father's arm and walked slowly across the lawn towards the wedding arch. Three rows of white chairs lined either side, each one occupied by a familiar smiling face, though she hardly saw them. Her gaze was captured by the man standing at the end of the aisle wearing the widest grin she'd ever seen. *Joshua. Her beloved.*

He took her breath away. She'd never seen him look so handsome, but her gaze was captivated by his dazzling blue eyes. Those eyes that pulled her in and kept her lost, were misty as she peered deeply into them.

"You look amazing," he whispered as her father placed her hand in his.

"So do you," she whispered back.

The anxiety disappeared. There was no doubt she was marrying the man of her dreams.

A grin remained permanently plastered on her face as the

ceremony proceeded. They exchanged vows and rings, and still, she couldn't stop smiling. Neither could Joshua. It was the strangest, most wonderful thing. Their joy was uncontainable.

When the pastor announced they were man and wife, Stella blinked several times. Already? Had they gotten to that part so soon?

"You may now kiss your bride," he stated.

Joyful tears pricked her eyes as Stella stepped towards her husband, reaching for him as he reached for her. Their lips met in a passionate kiss. Their first, as husband and wife. Applause ripped through the air as the sun's weakening rays shone down on them.

Their families gathered around with smiles and congratulations. It felt strange being the centre of attention, but with Joshua by her side, she didn't mind at all.

They greeted everyone in turn and accepted their congratulations. It was a long line and by the end of it, Stella was glad she opted for kitten heels instead of stilettos. Finally, Janella, the last in line, approached.

"Congratulations to both of you," she said, smiling. "I'm very happy for you. You make a stunning couple, but you already know that."

Stella's cheeks warmed in a blush. Knowing how Janella initially felt about their marriage, she was very happy to have her approval now. "Thank you, Janella. It means so much to us both to hear you say that."

She smiled. "I have a gift for you."

"A gift?" Joshua asked.

"Yes. It's inside. Would you come with me? It'll only take a moment. I'd like to give it to you personally."

Joshua and Stella glanced at each other. Their guests were waiting to mingle, drink and eat. They couldn't just slip away. Could they?

"I know you have other obligations, but I want to give you this before things get too crazy. Plus, I don't want anyone else to see it."

Now Stella was curious. "We can spare a minute," she said, lacing her fingers in Joshua's.

"Of course, Janella. Lead the way," he said.

"We'll be right back," Stella said in response to Elizabeth's quizzical frown.

They followed Janella to the house, and to her bedroom. What could she have to show them that she didn't want anyone else to see?

They arrived in the simple, but tastefully decorated room. Someone liked green; it was all over the place, along with dozens of photos depicting her family's lives. Stella smiled at a picture of Julian and Janella when they were young, but her attention turned to the centre of the room and a chair with a large white sheet covering it. There was something underneath, but what it could be, Stella had no idea.

"Joshua," Janella began. "I love you. I've loved you since we were children, and you became my little brother because you were Julian's brother. I've watched you grow up, and I've never been prouder of you. I know Julian would be, too, if he were here."

Stella faced her husband. His expression was still, but there was a slight quiver in his lips. "I love you too, Janella," he said in a thick voice.

She stepped closer. "I had this done in Kununurra. I

thought it would look good on some vacant wall," she said with a small laugh.

Stella was baffled by the statement but continued to listen.

"Your brother always wanted things to go back to the way they were, but he had a misguided plan of how it should get there. In honour of that desire, I want to present you and Stella with this gift. It's something for you to keep and remember the wonderful days of your childhood. Build on those, not on what happened in between then and now. I pray it will bring you joy."

Janella took hold of the sheet and with a quick movement, pulled it away. Stella gasped. Painted in meticulous perfection was a portrait of Julian, Olivia, and Joshua when they were children. It was beautiful. "You look about ten," Stella commented in wonder.

"Eleven," Joshua whispered. He squeezed her hand reflexively, and she turned to look at him. His bottom lip quivered visibly as his eyes moistened. "Thank you, Janella." He stepped forward and hugged her.

"You're more than welcome. Happy wedding day."

WHEN JANELLA PRESENTED HER GIFT, it was the last thing Joshua expected. The painting revived memories of happy times, when life was carefree and he and his siblings liked each other. There'd been so many wasted years in between that were filled with misunderstanding and anger. But this was a good memory, and he would treasure it forever.

"Are you okay, Joshua?" Stella asked as they left Janella's room. She clung to him and rubbed his arm.

"Yes," he replied. "I wish Julian could have been here today."

"We all do." She touched his cheek lightly. "I love you, Josh."

He gripped her hand and kissed the inside of her palm. "Thank you for being here for me, Stella. I love you more than you know."

"We have the rest of our lives for you to show me how much." She grinned.

He grinned, too, as he slipped his hand around her waist and pulled her close. "Since we've started with the gifts, there's no time like the present for my gift to you."

Stella's brow wrinkled. "A gift for me? I thought we decided not to exchange gifts."

"I got it before we made that decision," he stated. "Don't worry. You'll like it. No need to give me anything." He kissed her softly. "Now I have you, I have everything I need. Come on, let's go back to the party. I want everyone to see what I'm giving you."

"Joshua?" Stella said as he took her and led her down the hallway.

"Don't talk, just walk." The grin on his face grew larger, although his heart began to pound as he anticipated her reaction.

The presentation of his gift had to be delayed, however, but not by long. They had to do the customary couple's arrival and endure the pre-meal speeches. Thankfully, his father kept it brief, and so did most of the others who chose to speak.

Even Sean chose to say a few words. At first, Joshua was nervous, but as his cousin spoke, all concern disappeared. "I just want to say congratulations to a great couple. Stella, you've married the best guy I know. My cousin has always been the kind of guy you want to have beside you in a pinch. I wanted him to keep living the single life with me, but I realise that he's better off in a married life with you. I might not have said this before, but I ask your forgiveness for all the trouble I caused. I wish you and Joshua every happiness." He raised his champagne flute. "Congratulations!"

Everyone clapped, and finally it was Joshua's turn to speak. He stood, pushing his sleeves further up his arms, though they hadn't moved. It was habit. "Ladies and gentlemen, on behalf of my wife and me, I want to thank you all for being here to celebrate this momentous occasion in our lives. You have no idea how much it means to us, but be assured, it's a lot." He laughed while a chuckle rose amongst the guests.

He turned to Stella. "My darling wife. You've given me the greatest gift I could ask for by entrusting me with your future. I want you to know that I intend to do everything in my power to ensure you have everything you need and that the life we live will be the best life you could wish for."

Stella beamed at him.

Taking her hand, he pulled her gently to her feet as he continued. "Stella Goddard," he began, reaching into his breast pocket to retrieve the deed. He held the envelope in his hand and placed it in hers. "I know what you want most. Therefore, I give it to you."

Her forehead creased as she peered at the envelope.

"Open it," he urged, hardly able to contain his excitement.

She turned the envelope over and pulled out the folded paper, looking at him quizzically before unfolding it.

Joshua's grin widened as Stella began to read. Her breath hitched and tears welled in her eyes. "Joshua. It can't. You didn't. Oh, my!" She turned to her parents. "Mum. Dad. It's Indigo. Joshua's given me Indigo!"

"What?" Her father jumped to his feet and peered at the deed. Gloria stepped forward to hug Stella. They both shed tears.

Finally, Stella turned back to Joshua, eyes still glistening. "You crazy, wonderful man. I love you so much." She kissed him repeatedly. "Thank you. Thank you. Thank you!"

On cue, the song they'd chosen for their first dance began to play. He led her onto the dance floor, and taking her in his arms, deed still clutched in her hand, he slow danced her across the floor.

You ask how much I need you, must I explain?
I need you, oh my darling, like roses need rain.
You ask how long I'll love you; I'll tell you true:
Until the twelfth of never, I'll still be loving you.

CHAPTER 28

*F*rank sat holding Maggie's hand as everything transpired. Stella's reaction to the return of Indigo Downs was everything he imagined it would be. He was glad they were happy. He was glad that God saw it fit to not only bring Joshua and Stella together, but to return to her what had been lost. He smiled. *You are truly remarkable, Father.*

"Wonderful," Maggie whispered to him.

"Yes," he whispered back. He turned to her. Though the meal was yet to be served, couples were already filing onto the dance floor. Joshua and Stella had turned ceremony norms upside down, but no one was complaining. It wasn't an evening to stick to strict rules. It was a time to celebrate and enjoy.

Frank rose to his feet, pulling Maggie up beside him. If everyone was going to dance, why not them? He led her onto the dance floor. On the way, he spotted Elizabeth leading a very awkward looking Sean onto the floor with her. Frank smiled at his nephew and the apprehensive look on his face. Chuckling, he said to Maggie, "Look at that."

She looked in Sean's direction and smiled. "It looks like Elizabeth has him on a short leash," she mused.

"Indeed. That girl is a tidal wave. I like her."

"So do I," Maggie said.

They reached the dance floor, choosing a spot near the periphery. Frank took Maggie in his arms and held her close. He inhaled the scent of her hair, vanilla and brown sugar. "You smell delicious. I could eat you up."

"Is that so," she cooed. Her head was on his chest, and he knew she was listening to the beat of his heart. It was something she liked doing. He liked that she did it.

"Perhaps later," Frank teased, his voice low, a whisper against her ear. He kissed her earlobe.

Maggie slapped him playfully on the arm. "Frank, behave."

He laughed. He loved teasing her. "What? Can't I kiss my wife?"

"Yes, but not like that. At least not in public. You aren't a lovestruck teenager anymore," she said through a giggle.

"Why shouldn't I be? Why do the young get to have all the fun? I'm not that old. Neither are you. Are our days of glory over just because we have some grey hair on our heads? I say not. I say that, more than anyone, we have reason to rejoice."

She looked up at him adoringly. "You have some of the most charming ideas. Tell me, what might that reason be?"

"Because we've made it through the battle of life and marriage, not once, but twice," Frank replied. "Because I love you more each day. Because you make me feel young, and we want to make the most of our lives together." He grinned. "Do you need more? I can go on."

"No need," Maggie answered, her eyes moist.

He pulled her closer, pressing her against him. "God has surely blessed us, Maggie. The child I worried about is settled and more stable than I've ever seen him. Now a married man, and soon responsible for an entire station on his own."

"Are you worried about that? What he'll do without you there to guide him?"

"No. Joshua's lived his entire life on a cattle station. He knows what's required, even if he hasn't had full responsibility yet. It's in his blood. Any big issues, I'm sure he'll come to me, but I want him to have the room to be his own man. To be his own boss."

"I hoped you'd say that." Maggie smiled.

"Did you doubt I would?"

"No. I just wanted to hear you say it. Letting go isn't easy, especially with your children. You've never had your children leave home and stay away. I have. It was difficult for me to see Serena and Jeremy go off to live their lives. It can't be easy for you. You want them to be independent. We teach them that but watching them go is another thing. Part of you still wants to hold on."

Frank smiled. "How do you know me so well?"

She'd spoken directly to his heart, saying the things he felt but couldn't verbalise. He felt strange, just a little something, nothing worth considering, but the moment Maggie said it, every word rang true.

He hugged her. "I'm going to miss him."

She rubbed his back soothingly. "I know, but I'll help you through it."

"I feel a little silly feeling this way. Indigo isn't that far."

"But it's far enough. Enough to make you feel like an outsider looking in."

Frank sighed. "I haven't had to let them go like this before. After Esther, I tried to keep them close. I got Olivia back. Now I've lost Julian, and Joshua's leaving."

"You have me," Maggie said, lifting her gaze.

"Yes, I do, and I'm the most blessed man alive." Frank smiled, gazing into her eyes as they slow-danced to the music.

She rested her head against his chest. "I love you, Frank. I'm so glad I married you."

"And I'm glad I married you." He kissed her forehead while they continued dancing. The sun was slowly setting. Shards of orange melted into a purplish-blue, casting a soft light across the paddocks. Frank watched the sun drop below the horizon. It was like a message from God. One chapter was over, but a new one was beginning. There would be darkness, but there would be joy. Joshua and Stella were starting something new, and God would bless them. He knew it in his bones.

He looked around, finding his children and grandchildren in the crowd, noting their happy, smiling faces. Everything was as it should be. The world was at peace, at least at Goddard Downs. At least for now.

I pray this lasts forever, Lord. Smile on Goddard Downs. Smile on my family. Bless them. In Jesus' name. Amen.

∾

A NOTE FROM THE AUTHOR

I hope you enjoyed "Slow Dance at Dusk"! The Goddard family story continues in Book 5, "Slow Trek to Triumph". Read the first chapter below.

Enjoyed "Slow Dance at Dusk"? You can make a big difference. Help other people find this book by writing a review and telling them why you liked it. Honest reviews of my books help bring them to the attention of other readers just like yourself, and I'd be thrilled if you could spare just five minutes to leave a review (it can be as short as you like).

Blessings,

Juliette

SLOW TREK TO TRIUMPH (PREVIEW)

CHAPTER 1

*F*rank could hardly keep track of the changes occurring in his life and that of his family, but this latest change brought a smile to his lips every time he thought of it. His youngest son, Joshua, had married Stella and they were now living at Indigo Downs, the cattle station Stella's family had owned and lost, and which Joshua had purchased back for her as a wedding gift.

The couple had left for their honeymoon right after the wedding, and since then, Frank had resumed the role of managing Goddard Downs, a role he was more than familiar with. He was, however, finding it difficult to rouse himself each morning, something he'd never had a problem with before. Perhaps it was the lingering heartburn that had been troubling him in recent times, but more likely, it was simply that he didn't want to leave Maggie. Whenever his gaze settled on his beautiful wife's sleeping form, he was tempted to stay with her and not go to work. He was getting soft in his old age.

In the short time Joshua had been running things, Frank and Maggie had settled into a routine of long breakfasts on their deck, followed by a Bible reading and a prayer time. Returning to the helm had all but ended that. Maggie had been more than understanding and never grumbled or complained, but he knew she was missing their time together as much as he was.

But that morning, as he sat down for a quick breakfast, he made a decision. He took her hand across the table and rubbed it gently with his thumb.

She lifted her gaze and gave a bemused smile.

"My love," he said, "I think we should take that trip."

Her eyes shot open. "Now?"

"Yes." He looked deep into her eyes that flickered with confusion.

"What about the station? All the work that has to be done? We still haven't found a vet to replace Stella, nor an extra hand to help with the drives."

He lifted a finger to her lips and hushed her. "Shhh, my love. All those things can be figured out. We need to take time for each other while we can. The station will survive without me for a while." He squeezed her hand and lifted it to his lips, kissing it gently. "I want us to spend time together, Maggie. Just you and me, before we get too old. What do you say?"

She stared at him for a long moment, their gazes locked, before she replied, "I'd love to, Frank, so long as you truly think you can afford the time."

"I'll make sure I can." He smiled, the delight in her expression warming his heart. "Broome it is, then?"

She nodded eagerly. "Why don't we make a road trip of it?

I'd love to be able to take our time and enjoy all the sights along the way."

"Funny you should say that. I just happen to have been working on the perfect rig."

"Oh?" she said, her brows furrowing.

He chuckled. "Come down to the workshop later and I'll show you."

"Okay." She leaned forward and searched his eyes as her own danced with merriment. "How long have you been planning this, Frank?"

He grinned. "Since the day we met."

"Oh, go on with you, Frank Goddard. Seriously. How long?"

He leaned back in his chair and sipped his chamomile tea. He'd gone off coffee recently after finding that Maggie's herbal teas soothed him better. He'd even started enjoying the flavour. He stared out across the lagoon where a family of ducks was enjoying an early morning paddle.

When had he started planning this? Good question. Julian's sudden death had made him realise once again that no one, other than God, knew how many days they had left on this earth. That day as they lowered his eldest son's body into the ground, he'd made a decision to cherish every day, to take pleasure in life, and to spend as much time with Maggie and his family as he possibly could. He didn't want to live his life with regret.

He faced her and drew a slow breath. "Since Julian's funeral."

Her expression sobered and an understanding passed between them. Words weren't needed. She knew how much

Julian's death had affected him, but God was gracious, and although he'd never fully get over his son's death, he, along with the rest of the family, was learning to live without him.

"I'll make some more tea," she said.

He smiled. "Thank you, my love. That would be great, and then maybe we can do a bit of planning before I head off. I told Liv I'd be in late this morning."

"Okay. I'll grab my notebook and laptop." Maggie returned a few seconds later with both items and sat beside him. He could hardly get a word in as she began to explore the possible routes, expounding on the pros and cons of each. She was so meticulous, and she had the best photo spots and attractions brought up within minutes, suggesting the places they could stop on their way to and from Broome, the seaside town where they'd honeymooned three years before.

"But when we get there, we'll have to stay in the same hotel we did for our honeymoon." She lifted her gaze from her screen and met his. Unspoken words passed between them.

Recalling those magical days and nights, their first as husband and wife, brought a smile to his lips. With its long sandy beaches and laidback lifestyle, Broome was the absolute best place for a honeymoon. But it was also a great place to camp. He made circles on her hand with his thumb. "Oh, I thought we'd camp."

Her eyes widened and disappointment flashed across her face until he chuckled. "I'm only kidding, my love. The hotel it is."

Her face broke into a relieved smile as she swatted him gently on the arm. "Frank. You do like to tease, don't you?"

He reached out and curled a loose tendril of hair around his finger before slipping his hand behind her head and drawing her face close to brush his lips across hers. "But I like this more."

Laughing, she returned his kiss before pushing to her feet. "You'll be fired if you don't get to work soon."

He grinned. "Bring it on!"

"You don't mean that, Frank."

"No, but I'm looking forward to taking some time off."

"So am I. It'll be wonderful." She wrapped her arms around his neck from behind and kissed his cheek. "Now, off you go."

He squeezed her hands and angled his head to smile at her. "Come down later and we'll tell the family."

"But we haven't decided anything definite yet."

"We've decided we're going. That's enough. And they'll need time to prepare for when we're gone."

She nodded. "You're right. I'll pop down a little later and you can show me the rig as well."

"You're going to love it." A grin grew on his face as he imagined her reaction when she saw the camper he'd been secretly working on for weeks.

She chuckled and ruffled his hair. "I'm sure I will."

AFTER FRANK LEFT, Maggie tidied away the dishes and made another cup of tea. Her mind was awhirl. She needed a few quiet moments to process what had just happened. With Julian's passing and Joshua moving to Indigo Downs, she'd assumed the trip she and Frank had been talking about since their wedding would be put off indefinitely. While she was okay with that, because Goddard Downs was his life after all, it had also saddened her. Spending time together, just the two of them, exploring new places, was something she'd looked forward to, but she was wise enough to know that best made plans often didn't happen. So Frank's announcement that he wanted to go anyway filled her with excitement and gratitude.

She carried her tea to the deck, and after easing into her chair, she opened her Bible to do her morning reading. Although she was studying the book of Hebrews, she opened it at her favourite Psalm, Psalm 100, and read it aloud, softly.

Shout for joy to the Lord, all the earth.
Worship the Lord with gladness;
come before Him with joyful songs.
Know that the Lord is God.
It is He who made us, and we are His;
we are His people, the sheep of His pasture.
Enter His gates with thanksgiving
and His courts with praise;
give thanks to Him and praise His name.
For the Lord is good and His love endures forever;
His faithfulness continues through all generations.

Like the psalmist, Maggie's heart overflowed with gratitude for the many blessings God had bestowed on her. She took a deep breath and closed her eyes. *Lord, I give You thanks for Your goodness. For bringing me to this place where I know beyond a shadow of a doubt You want me to be, but I also give You praise that Frank and I can spend quality time together while experiencing Your amazing creation. Go before us and prepare the way for Goddard*

Downs to run without Frank. Bless the family and raise them up to be the people You want them to be. I pray these things in Your Son's precious name. Amen.

An hour later, she wandered down to the workshop. It was that time of year when the ground was beginning to cry out for rain, and she had to be careful where she walked as deep ruts had started to appear in the track. Once the rains came and the dirt became soft and pliable, the boys would grade the tracks, levelling them out and making them easier to traverse, although she wasn't sure which she preferred. Dirt or mud. She chuckled. How her thoughts had changed in the three years she'd lived here. She'd loved city life, but there was something special about living on the land. God seemed closer somehow. She knew that wasn't the case since God was everywhere, so she guessed the change was in her. She had more time to appreciate His goodness, to see His hand at work, and choosing to walk instead of driving the short distance gave her that extra time.

Her heart was light by the time she reached the large workshop where all the vehicle maintenance was carried out. By necessity, Frank had learned to change an engine, fix a gearbox, and he could troubleshoot almost any mechanical fault a vehicle might have. Julian had never learned those skills. He'd preferred someone else look after that messy part of the business. Joshua had taken an interest, but preferred looking after the horses. Nate, Olivia's husband, being city born and bred, was not mechanically inclined at all, and Sean, Frank's nephew, wasn't reliable enough. But David, Serena's husband, was a firefighter who didn't mind getting his hands dirty and was still trying to find his place at Goddard Downs. Frank had told

Maggie that he hoped he might pass his knowledge onto David over time, but it was looking more and more likely they'd have to employ a mechanic from outside the family. And sooner than later, if she and Frank were to take this trip. Another thing to hand over to God.

She poked her head into the workshop and frowned. Frank didn't seem to be there. In fact, it was so quiet she could hear the ticking of the clock on the far wall. She took a breath and a swig of water and was turning to walk up to the main house when her gaze caught sight of the rig. Her eyes widened, and then she laughed. She'd assumed Frank had fixed the old caravan they'd bought not long after they married, but this wasn't the caravan. It was a camper that fitted onto the back of a small truck, much like a tortoise carrying its home with it wherever it went. She'd seen them on the road, of course. Tourists travelled through the Kimberley in the dry season sporting all sorts of rigs, and she'd always thought a camper like this would be fun. And now, as she stepped closer and studied it, she thought it was the perfect setup for her and Frank. It wasn't large by any means, but it would give them the best of both worlds. Indoor sleeping and outdoor living, and they wouldn't have to drag a van over those corrugated dirt roads. She was investigating the slide out stove when footsteps sounded from behind. Turning, she came face to face with Frank.

His eyes danced as he searched hers. "What do you think, my love?"

"I think it's perfect." Smiling, she walked into his embrace and leaned against his strong chest.

He kissed the top of her head. "I think so, too. Let me show you inside."

"Frank." She chuckled at the suggestive tone of his voice. "I've already looked, and it's very cosy. I might even pass on the hotel, but right now, don't we have a family meeting to get to?"

He released a heavy sigh. "Yes, we do." He slipped an arm around her shoulders. "So, you like it?"

She looked into his eyes. "I love it. And I love that you want to do this trip. I can't wait to be travelling the open road with you."

He rubbed her arm. "We'd better go and break the news."

"Yes, we should."

They strolled the half kilometre to the homestead, chatting about where they would head to first, and what they'd need to take to last several weeks on the road before reaching any shops where they could restock. While joy bubbled through her, Maggie's mind whirled. There was so much to think about it. How could they carry enough food to last three weeks? What about cooking utensils? And what clothes should they take?

"It's all in hand, my love. I asked Janella to order extra supplies this month. We're ready to go as soon as we tell the family."

"Oh Frank. I can't believe you kept this from me."

He chuckled. "I wanted it to be a surprise."

She laughed as she leaned into him. "You definitely succeeded."

～

THE FAMILY WAS GATHERED in the main house. Everyone, including Joshua and Stella, was present, and it was a welcome sight to Frank's eyes. Although the couple now lived four hours' drive away, they'd agreed to attend the monthly family business meetings, and this was the first since their wedding.

"Good morning," Frank said brightly, looking at each face around the table. Maggie sat to his right, Serena and David were beside her, Olivia and Nate sat opposite, Joshua and Stella were at the other end, Sean sat beside Joshua, and Janella was to Frank's left. Sasha was minding the younger children who were playing quietly in the adjoining room. His granddaughter possessed a natural maternal instinct that her cousins responded to. They were always happy to have her look after them.

"First, I'd like to thank you all for being here, and a big welcome back to Joshua and Stella." As he gave the newlyweds a nod, a wave of pride swept through him. The change in Joshua since Julian's death was nothing less than remarkable, and although they all missed Julian greatly, God had used his death to work in Joshua's life, changing him from a troubled young man who had little idea of what he wanted, to a responsible, mature husband and leader.

"We have a lot of business to cover this morning, but before we begin, let's start with a word of prayer."

They joined hands and bowed their heads as Frank committed their time to the Lord. "Dear Lord and Heavenly Father, Thank You for Joshua's and Stella's safe return. We ask that You bless our time together and guide us as we make decisions that will affect us all. In Your precious Son's name. Amen."

After taking a sip of tea, Frank turned to Joshua. "How are things at Indigo? Settling in okay?"

Joshua crossed his arms. "Yes, but we need to find some hands before we get the new herd. We've put the word out but haven't advertised yet. We'd rather try for hands we've at least heard of before looking for new ones."

Frank nodded approvingly. "Good idea."

"Less time training, too," Stella chimed in. "We want to get the new herd settled well before the next rainy season."

"Indeed," Frank agreed. "Speaking of which," he squeezed Maggie's hand, "we have an announcement."

As expected, all eyes turned to him.

"What is it, Dad?" Olivia folded her arms and studied him with narrowed eyes, her gaze darting between him and Maggie. He'd known that his daughter would have the most issue with them disappearing for a few weeks, so he replied to her.

"Maggie and I have decided to take a trip."

Olivia frowned. "Now? With everything that needs to be done?"

He nodded. "Yes. I've thought and prayed long and hard about this. Maggie and I need some time alone, and I'm sure you'll survive without us for a while." Breaking his gaze with Olivia, he looked around the table, his gaze taking in each of the other family members in turn. "We'd love you all to work together to ensure everything runs smoothly while we're gone."

"How long are you going for?" Olivia barked.

"We haven't fully decided, but perhaps a month. Once we

have a better idea, we'll let you know. We just wanted to give you a heads-up so we can start getting things ready to leave."

"But we still have to find a vet to replace Stella, and some new hands..." she continued.

"You're more than capable of handling all of that, Olivia." He raised a brow and gave a pointed look.

She huffed out a breath and shook her head but remained silent.

Usually, he would never have contemplated taking an extended trip with so many tasks outstanding, but things had changed. He cast his gaze around the table. "This will be a time for you all to step up. To learn some new skills. To work together. I have confidence in you all, and I know you'll be fine." He placed his hands on the table. "That's all I have to share on my end other than saying I expect to have an update from Mr. Tamala sometime soon, but Joshua and Stella will be handling that arrangement going forward since the new herd will be under their supervision."

He didn't miss how his statement caused the corners of Joshua's lips to rise in a half-grin, half-smile. His son needed his space, an opportunity to shine, not only as a man, but as a husband and as head of his own house. Frank was glad they'd finally come to a place where they could each be the men they were meant to be. It was long in coming. Julian would have been proud to see how his younger brother had stepped up already. That thought caused Frank's heart to feel heavy. It wasn't that long ago Julian was chairing these family meetings, eager to show himself as responsible. He never had anything to prove in Frank's eyes, but he didn't seem to understand that.

Frank handed the floor to Joshua who proceeded to explain

the process they were undertaking to select the new herd. Stella added her points on the selection process and stated that she would be personally choosing the new cattle, especially the studs, whose breeding prowess would improve the herd's quality for years to come.

Finally, once those matters were settled and everyone's questions answered, Frank opened the floor to any other business. "Does anyone else have anything to say?"

"I do," David said quickly, sitting straighter and clearing his throat.

Silence fell on the room before Frank nodded. "Good. The floor's yours. Over to you."

"Thanks." David smiled as his gaze swept around the table. "Good morning to everyone. As newcomers, Serena and I don't have much to contribute normally, but there's a matter which I believe affects us all and is about to directly impact Serena."

Leaning forward, Frank crossed his arms on the table and pinned David with his gaze. "Newcomers or not, you're family, and that gives you a right to speak."

David gave an appreciative, and a relieved, smile. "Thank you."

"So, what seems to be the trouble?" Frank asked.

David released a heavy sigh. "It's the rains. We've only had one Christmas here, but in that time, we got to see how isolated Goddard Downs becomes during the wet season, and how dangerous it can be. Serena's programme with the children is doing well, and this place is a sanctuary for them, but if they can't come during the rainy season because it's not safe to travel, everything she's been trying to do with them could be derailed. Months without being able to come could do more harm than good."

"What do you have in mind?" Frank asked.

"A bridge."

Everyone's eyes widened and an audible gasp rounded the table.

David continued quickly. "I'm suggesting we build a bridge to provide safe passage to and from Goddard Downs, eliminating its isolation during the wet season. Having a bridge will also help in an emergency."

"And it would mean the children can come here safely all year round," Serena added. "They already experience so many disappointments, I don't want to add to them."

Frank took a slow breath. He'd raised the idea of a bridge years before when his father still held the reins, but the idea had been vetoed because of the cost. Now, however, the station was in a much better financial position. He glanced at Maggie. She'd been silently listening and met his gaze, hope filling her eyes. The project with the children had helped Serena overcome her own issues, and Maggie would welcome the idea of a bridge if it would help both her daughter and the children.

He faced David and gave a nod. "I like the idea."

"A bridge, Dad? Really?" Olivia protested, leaning forward. "Don't get me wrong, I'm all for anything that would make the station safer and enable Serena to carry on her programme, but we're talking about building something that none of us have any idea how to do, nor of the costs involved. It could cost more than it's worth." She folded her arms and sat back in her chair with a stony expression on her face.

Of course, Olivia would be negative. "We won't know that

until we investigate," Frank replied, trying not to be too conde-scending. "How do the rest of you feel?"

Janella spoke first. "I think it's a great suggestion. I've always thought something needed to be done. I think we all have at one point or another, but no one ever said anything."

"It's because we're used to it," Frank said. "We've grown up with the rains and the flooding, and we've just accepted that's the way it is. David and Serena haven't." He nodded at the pair. "Sometimes new eyes are all that's needed to find a solution. Sean, what do you think?"

Blinking, his nephew straightened and ran his hand across his shaggy hair. "Ah… I…I think it's about time. I could help."

"How are you going to help with that broken arm?" Olivia asked almost derisively before turning her gaze to Frank. "I think we should stick a pin in the entire thing until we have more information to base a decision on."

"We aren't deciding now, Liv," Frank said, holding her gaze. "But yes, we need information. David, can I entrust you to undertake some research?"

"Certainly. I'll make a few calls and see what the process would be."

Olivia drew a long breath and blew it out. She sat forward in her chair. "Okay. I'll get some quotes and see just how much this idea will cost, although I think it's going to be more than we can afford. We'd have to engage engineers and get the land surveyed, and then we'd have to find a construction company who could build it, plus pay for all the materials, and it wouldn't be a small bridge."

Frank smiled. His daughter would do a thorough job of gathering details, even if she didn't support the idea. "Perhaps you and David can work together and report back at the next meeting. I'm thinking we should call an interim one before Maggie and I leave. Five days to put everything together?"

Olivia's eyes shot open. "Five days? That's not long enough."

"We need things to move quickly. I want to have this matter tabled or actioned before Maggie and I leave. A week from today should be enough time."

"At least that's better than five days," Olivia said, rolling her eyes. "Are we done?"

"I think so, unless anyone else has something they want to raise?" Frank waited a moment, and when no one responded, he called the meeting to an end.

MAGGIE RETURNED to the cottage to start planning their trip while Frank settled into his office for the day. He was pleased with how things had gone at the meeting, although there'd been little to debate other than the bridge. David's idea was a good one and worth investigating. If it proceeded, it would be another change, but one that Frank would welcome. He was more than used to the access issues the station experienced during the wet season, but having vehicular access all year round had to be beneficial.

Order your copy to continue reading Book 5, Slow Trek to Triumph

OTHER BOOKS BY JULIETTE DUNCAN

Find all of Juliette Duncan's books on her websites:

www.julietteduncan.com/library

www.julietteduncanbookstore.com

Beneath the Southern Cross: The Dawn of a Sunburned Land Series

Love's Unwavering Hope

Love's Rebellious Spirit

Love's Distant Dream

Love's Precious Moments

Love's Faithful Journey (Coming 2026)

A Sunburned Land Series

Slow Road to Love

Slow Path to Peace

Slow Ride Home

Slow Dance at Dusk

Slow Trek to Triumph

Christmas at Goddard Downs

True Love Series

Tender Love

Tested Love

Tormented Love

Triumphant Love

Precious Love Series

Forever Cherished

Forever Faithful

Forever His

Water's Edge Series

When I Met You

Because of You

With You Beside Me

All I Want is You

It Was Always You

My Heart Belongs to You

I'm Loving You

Finding You Under the Mistletoe

The Shadows Series

Lingering Shadows

Facing the Shadows

Beyond the Shadows

Secrets and Sacrifice

A Highland Christmas

A Time For Everything Series

A Time to Treasure

A Time to Care

A Time to Abide

A Time to Rejoice

Freed by His Love

ABOUT THE AUTHOR

Juliette Duncan is passionate about writing true to life Christian romances that will touch her readers' hearts and make a difference in their lives. Drawing on her own often challenging real-life experiences, Juliette writes deeply emotional stories that highlight God's amazing love and faithfulness, for which she's eternally grateful. Juliette lives on the beautiful Sunshine Coast of Queensland, Australia, and she and her husband have five adult children and eleven grandchildren. When not writing, Juliette and her husband love exploring the great outdoors.

Connect with Juliette:

Email: author@julietteduncan.com

Website: www.julietteduncan.com

Juliette's bookstore: www.julietteduncanbookstore.com

Facebook: www.facebook.com/JulietteDuncanAuthor

BookBub: www.bookbub.com/authors/juliette-duncan